A
THOUSAND
BLUE

For Amy

Even though you're mental, you are still one of my favourite people in the whole wide world!

A THOUSAND BLUE

With love,

STUART FINNIE

Copyright © 2012 Stuart Finnie

The moral right of the author has been asserted.

Apart from any fair dealing for the purposes of research or private study, or criticism or review, as permitted under the Copyright, Designs and Patents Act 1988, this publication may only be reproduced, stored or transmitted, in any form or by any means, with the prior permission in writing of the publishers, or in the case of reprographic reproduction in accordance with the terms of licences issued by the Copyright Licensing Agency. Enquiries concerning reproduction outside those terms should be sent to the publishers.

Matador
9 Priory Business Park
Kibworth Beauchamp
Leicestershire LE8 0RX, UK
Tel: (+44) 116 279 2299
Fax: (+44) 116 279 2277
Email: books@troubador.co.uk
Web: www.troubador.co.uk/matador

ISBN 978 1780880 983

British Library Cataloguing in Publication Data.
A catalogue record for this book is available from the British Library.

Typeset in 11pt Book Antiqua by Troubador Publishing Ltd, Leicester, UK

Matador is an imprint of Troubador Publishing Ltd

Printed and bound in the UK by TJ International, Padstow, Cornwall

For Mara McWhirter...
...My very best friend.

And memories, he knew, were not glass treasures to be kept locked within a box. They were bright ribbons to be hung in the wind.

The Talismans of Shannara — Terry Brooks

1

A windless cold nipped at her exposed cheeks; her breath swirled as silver mist in the air and then vanished before her. Plastic shopping bags, heavy with food for tonight's meal, bit sharply into her gloves. The scrape of her heels on the pavement, the rumble of cars as they slid by and the chatter of passing strangers went unnoticed to her. Her thoughts were given to the events of the next few hours, and of how he would react to her news.

Under the glow of a streetlight she stopped, resting the bags on the ground, letting the blood return to her numbed fingers. She arched her back, loosening the muscles in her neck and shoulders. Her breathing remained heavy, but in another half mile she would be home. She stiffened the collar of her coat and pulled her woolly hat down further over the tips of her ears. Stars were out, she knew, but they were invisible, lost in the cloudless sky beyond the thick orange haze overhead: a sky that would allow the temperature to fall even further below freezing through the night. By morning her world would be sugar-coated white with frost but by then nothing in their lives would be the same. She wondered if they would sleep.

Children were already out in groups, ringing bells and knocking on doors. Squeals of delight filled the cold October air as handfuls of sweets and chocolates were gratefully accepted by witches and devils, by superheroes and princesses. She caught herself smiling as they giggled their way round each neighbour, remembering for a moment what it was like to be that age; remembering the simplicity, the beauty, the innocence.

The bags seemed heavier now after her short rest but she continued on nonetheless. Dinner was to be served at nine; he'd be home around eight thirty, and would open the door to the aroma of his favourite meal. He'd know right away there was something unusual – she had only cooked for him once before, on his birthday – but he would play his part and say nothing until she did. She would slide the card across to him, and confused, he'd open it. She imagined his eyes as he read the words, the glow of a single candle catching the gentle contours of his face. He would smother her in kisses. He would promise to be with her to the end. She hoped more than anything, he would be.

Then, a scream; it sounded like nothing she had ever heard before. She looked across the road to see a child dressed as a pirate run out between parked cars, and be lit up by the headlights of an oncoming vehicle. Her eyes met the mothers': Sophie; she knew her. Another scream, only this time tyres sliding on tarmac; then the child stopped, petrified as he saw the danger. An outstretched hand was all Sophie could do; her mouth agape as terror swallowed her. In Sophie's eyes, she saw helplessness. In Sophie's scream, she heard loss. And in Sophie's stillness, she knew what she must do.

Chapter One

We live in my grandmother's house. It's a tired, damp two bedroom apartment in a run-down tenement block and although it will be years later before I learn why I live the first few years of my life here, I love it. Orange carpets worn almost bare; torn woodchip wallpaper painted and stained different shades of brown; hideous wooden panelling above a fireplace that doesn't work; an ancient kitchen that smells of stale milk; a cold and grey bathroom; the deathly sound of silence and the looks of dread that flashed between my family whenever my grandfather would stagger drunk through the door – all images branded onto my infant brain by time's iron. But of all the memories, happy or otherwise, it's the night of August 25th I remember most of all. It is the night my little sister is born.

I make a noise with my spoon on my plate, scraping the stray flakes of cereal into the last of the milk the way my mum does. More than once I'm told to be quiet, but I'm only little – my third birthday is still two months away – and I like the sound it makes. Eventually, with adult patience worn out, I am sent to bed.

Something wakens me: All the lights are on; there's shouting from the front room, voices I don't recognise; scary blue lights spin on the walls; my uncle races round, telling me to stay in bed, stuffing towels and clothes into a plastic bag; my mum cries because my dad isn't there; a nice lady in a shiny yellow jacket wipes my tears away; "Everything will be just fine," she says before she helps my mum out into the dark, where they both disappear down the stairs; and then the long, deep quiet that follows as the door closes.

My gran comes in to my room, her breath warm on my cheek as she kisses me. She plays with my curly red hair, whispering what just happened. She always looks old, but right now the deep wrinkles and dark circles round her eyes have melted like midday snow. And she has a look on her face that I don't understand; a look both happy and sad at the same time. I cling to her, scared because they have taken my mum away and confused because I don't know who those people were in the house. But I'm also excited, very excited – tomorrow my gran says she will take me to the hospital to see my mum, on the bus.

She sits with me for a long time before my eyes grow heavy and she kisses me goodnight. As I'm falling asleep, as my baby sister screams her way into life and as our family grows, I smile... because tonight, in bed, I'm allowed to keep my socks on.

~

I am four years old.

It's a Sunday and the smell of a roast dinner cooking on the kitchen fills my house. Usually, I like to guess what vegetables we'll have, but I'm not in the mood today. I've been waiting in the living room, out of my mum's way like she told me to, but it's been ages and now I want to speak with her. I pop my head around the door. It's noisy, like it always is. Steam pours from silver pots on the cooker, escaping through the open window. The net curtain lifts and falls with the wind; it's beckoning me, daring me, to enter. Cold water runs in a steady stream from the tap, and a tub of pink ice-cream – strawberry, I hope – sits defrosting on the work surface. My stripy-pyjama panda is on the floor under the table and I want to go and get it. I look at my mum. She has her back to me. I think about saying something so she hears me. The curtain taunts me once more. My heart tightens. I want to cry.

A few nights ago, she read me a story. I knew it by heart, as I'd heard it since I was two, but at the end, when the hero fires one last arrow into the sky and whispers with his dying breath the word "goodbye" to his love, I asked her why he couldn't just come back to life. It was the first time I had ever asked her such a question. There was a look on her face I'd never seen before: Tiredness? Surprise? Loneliness? But the answer she gave made me break inside.

"When you die – and everyone dies – that's it. You're dead. No coming back." She spoke without looking at me.

"Even you?" I asked. She nodded. "And dad?" She nodded. "And me? Will I die too?" Again, she nodded. "What if I never say goodbye? Will that keep everyone alive?" Her silence was like a wall of stone. I felt tears gather behind my eyes. I tried to speak, to ask her for some reassurance, but I couldn't bring myself to talk. My fingers rubbed at my palms, needing a mothers' comfort, needing to feel. And then, her cold eyes still unable to meet me, she stood and left the room, closing the door behind her to leave me alone in the dark.

I feel those same tears well in my eyes now as she turns to face me. I look at her, at the confusion on her face. I want to cry out to her. I want her to tell me she'll never leave me; I am four years old and I need my mum to hold me and say she'll always be there for me. I need her to tell me she won't ever die. I open my mouth to speak, but all I can do is sob. My eyes haven't left hers. Her expression changes with my sadness. She moves toward me very quickly and I hold my arms out. I close my eyes and wait for her hug.

A sudden, sharp stinging on my leg sends a howl of pain from my open lips.

"Grow up," she says, and grabs me by the arm, forcing me back into the living room. "What's the matter with you now?"

I open my eyes and through the tears, I see the face of the woman who means more to me than anything else in the world. I want to tell her how much I love her; I want her to know I hope she lives with me forever, because I won't know how to survive without her; I want to tell my mum I love her.

But I can't speak. My leg stings, my throat hurts from the squeal I let out, and my eyes burn from the tears. "I'm sorry, mum," escapes from my throat as a whimper. "I'm sorry." She storms back into the kitchen to finish making dinner. I sit on the couch, alone, trying hard not to make any more noise. I don't know where to look. I want my panda.

She never knew what she did to me that day, my mum. We never spoke about it.

I am four years old, and I am alone in the world.

2

She opened her hands and let the bags fall from her grip; she heard the muffled thud and the sound of breaking glass as they hit the pavement. The wine, she thought: Californian red, his favourite, leaking blood-like all over the steak and potatoes and frozen dessert. She would not be making him dinner tonight. Not tonight, or any other night. Not now. She wondered if the card was such a good idea after all.

Stars blinked in the deep black overhead. A thin, white coating of frost covered everything around her, sparkling like tiny diamonds as light from a hundred sources reflected on its surface. How wonderful the world seemed to her then, how calm, how complete. A long breath slid into the night; an opaque fog, dancing, spiralling before fading to forever. The cold clawed at her face, stinging her cheeks, sending a lonely strand of saltwater down towards the corner of her mouth. Time had all but slowed to a stop.

Eye contact remained – shock, helplessness, fear. The mother, the boy-pirate, the oncoming car, the icy road, and the certainty of what she was about to do: each as vivid as the other, each one blending seamlessly together into a single fluid image in her mind.

The ground beneath her feet was solid. Her legs tensed as she leaned forward. A mixture of screams pierced the night, but none were hers. She thought again of the wine, of the dinner that she would not make. And then she moved.

Pushing off with her right foot, she leapt onto the road and into the bright glare of headlights. She covered the distance to the boy-

pirate in three strides, her eyes not leaving his for a moment. She wanted him to know everything would be fine, that no matter what happened, he would be all right. She didn't even have time to reassure him with a smile. Her white-gloved hands appeared before her in a blur and she swept the boy-pirate into her arms, turning her back on the dazzling light and the steady, unending screech of skidding tyres.

"Save him," she murmured. "Please save him."

Chapter Two

During the long summer break between the third and fourth years of primary school, my sister and I are bundled off to a holiday camp with our aunt and uncle. Two weeks by the sea; two weeks of building sandcastles; two weeks of playing in parks and getting ice-cream from shops along the waterfront – bliss! We are staying in a wooden lodge and in the brochure it has a picture of bunk-beds. Louise has just turned five and thinks she is a big girl, so she and I spend the days leading up to the trip arguing over who was sleeping on the top.

Before we leave, we kiss Ben goodbye and pay more attention than usual to our only pet. Even for a Border collie, he is beyond energetic, and my parents spend most of their time shouting at him for chewing furniture and clothes or for barking at birds through the window or for running away whenever the opportunity presents itself. But we adore him, my little sister and me. When she was really small, he used to let her ride his back, my dad holding her arms in case she fell, and he loved it. There are photos of him all over the house. He's part of our family. He's the brother we wanted and never had.

My aunt is my friend. She says if there's anything I ever want to talk about, I just need to ask her; I often do. My uncle is funny and very, very silly. He always tries to make me laugh, especially when I pretend to be sad. He'll tickle Louise and me until we can't move, and he'll sneak us both biscuits and sweets when no one is looking. I'd never say it to anyone, but he's definitely my favourite.

One night, halfway through the holiday, we are allowed to stay up late, as there is a show on the television that has our favourite singers and comedians on it. It seems very important, with red carpets and bright lights and it's held in a fancy theatre. My aunt sits on the couch with one arm around me, the other around my sister and we snuggle close. I look at my aunt and uncle, laughing at them laughing, still too young to understand most of the humour. My sister joins in. The noise is beautiful. Happiness, I decide, sounds like laughter.

Later, much later than I ever remember being up before, I climb the ladders to the top bunk and crawl under the covers. The muscles in my cheeks hurt. Below me, already tucked in and fast asleep, my sister gently smacks her lips together, tasting something only her dreams will ever know. My aunt kisses my forehead and switches the light off as she closes the door. I'm still smiling, breathing in the warmth, savouring the moment as my eyelids slip shut, and one shade of black replaces another.

After a time, I awake to the dreadful sound of a child's scream. Something doesn't feel right, and although it is still dark, I know I am no longer in my bed. I feel pain across my face and it's then I realise the scream I hear comes from my own mouth.

The light comes on and both my aunt and uncle rush in to see what's happening. I look down at the carpet. There is blood everywhere, and I scream louder. Louise wakens up, and immediately starts to cry. My aunt scoops her up in her arms and takes her through to her bed; my uncle lifts me and looks at me with deep, grey eyes. I continue to cry, but seeing him before me means I'll be okay. He strokes my face, hushing me, and reassuring me I'll be fine. I begin to choke on my own tears and my uncle holds me close and carries me into the main room of the lodge. He grabs a handful of tissues from a box and asks me to hold them tightly against my bleeding nose. Tilting my head back, he tells me of the time, when he was around my age, he fell out his bed, too, and I feel better knowing we share something, knowing he knows how I feel. Between tears, between shallow breaths, I thank him.

A few minutes later, my aunt brings Louise through to see me. She is holding my old stripy-pyjama panda and is sucking her thumb. The blood has been cleaned from my face. I'm sitting on the floor, my head tilted back and wads of tissue paper still packing my nose. Louise runs towards me, burying her head in my shoulder, her arms wrapping tightly round my back. I smile. I love my little sister more than anything in the world, and with one arm, I hold her close to me. My aunt grins at me from across the room and tells me that the bed-guard has been put back on to stop me falling out again. I ask Louise if she wants to swap with me, and she can have a turn sleeping on the top bunk. Without lifting her head, she shakes it vigorously, and with her cutest voice says, "No, no, no!"

I laugh, which hurts, and my aunt laughs too. My uncle walks into the room and asks what we're all laughing at. Louise shakes her head, again, and says "No, no, no!" and I laugh harder. So does my aunt. My uncle shrugs his shoulders and stares at us all. "Women," he mutters as he comes over to us. With ease, he scoops up my sister and tickles her. She squeals and tries to escape. "Save me!" she yells and reaches out to me; he laughs like the bad-guy from a cartoon and runs into the kitchen with her. The sound of Louise laughing makes my aunt and I laugh even more. "Save me! Save me!" she shouts, but we both know she doesn't want saving. My nose is still sore, but it's stopped bleeding. My aunt comes to sit with me, and slides her arm around my shoulder, holding me close. I lean my head against her chest and close my eyes.

It's strange how close we all are, here, without my mum

and dad, without schoolwork and friends, without my dolls and games. I think how much I want it to be this way forever. Amidst the sounds of laughter and thoughts of happiness, I yawn. I cuddle in closer to my aunt.

"Do you think you and Louise would like to sleep with us in our bed tonight?" she asks. I nod. In spite of the pain that burns across my face, I never want this night to end.

As the last moments of consciousness slip from me, I hear my sister laugh from the kitchen.

"Save me!" she yells. "Please someone save me!"

~

The drive home is sad.

Louise and I have spent the last two weeks being treated to every luxury we wanted. We went on donkey-back rides; we had a turn on a roller-coaster; we ate fish & chips for dinner every night, and sometimes even for lunch, too; we got candy-floss and sweets and fizzy juice in paper cups with bendy straws. And we never fought or argued. Not once. But now we were heading home, back to our mum and dad, back to everything normal.

We bought everyone a present from the holiday, with our own money. For my mum, we got a little porcelain house, painted in lots of lovely colours, with a tiny clock above the door that actually works and an old lady tending the flowers at the front. It was Louise who picked it; she said the lady looked like our gran, who was in heaven now. I agree with her. For my dad, we got a glass for his beer, with "world's best drinker" on it. And for Ben, we got a chewy bone that squeaks.

My uncle turns the car into the street where we live, and from the back seat, my sister and I see our mum at the window, watching for us, smiling and waving when she sees us. The car stops outside our house and Louise is first up the path. The door opens and my mum bends down to pick her up. Seconds behind her, I hug my mum's waist and she places her hand on top of my head.

"I've missed you, mummy!" Louise says and the smile on my mum's face beams joy as her two girls cling to her. "We got presents for you and daddy."

She wants to know everything about our holiday, and Louise and I talk over each other, telling her all the things we did in the kind of detail only children remember. I show her my nose, asking if she can tell it was bleeding. Louise shows her the numerous scrapes and bruises on her legs – battle-scars from pavements and beaches and playgrounds. The sun comes out from behind a grey cloud, and bathes us in its warmth. I find myself smiling. I'm glad to be home.

My uncle brings our luggage up the path and sits it in the hallway. I look over my mum's shoulder into the house. Something's not right. He kisses his sister on the cheek, gets back into the car, and together, the three of us wave to him and his wife as they drive away. I could swear my aunt is crying.

The house is silent. Something is definitely not right.

"Do you want your present now?" Louise asks. I slip past them into the living room. Everything is tidier and cleaner than I have ever seen it, even at Christmas time, when my mum makes us all help her to clear up. The window is open, but there is no sound from outside, just the faintest breeze crawling across the carpet to breathe on my skin. It's all so quiet. Why is it so quiet?

And then it hits me.

"Mum," I ask. "Where's Ben?"

We stare at each other. No words pass between us.

Louise shouts on him, singing his name and clucking her tongue against the roof of her mouth the way my dad does, expecting him to come bounding into her in an explosion of energy. But he doesn't come. My mum walks into the kitchen, sits at the dining table and tells Louise and me to sit with her. She has something to tell us.

"He's gone," she says, after explaining how he ran out of the open gate and vanished down the street. Her and my dad searched for him for hours, but couldn't find him, she says. She reaches across and holds Louise's hand.

"Maybe he'll come back when he's hungry," I say, numbed by her words.

"No," she says. "He won't be coming back."

"Maybe he was out looking for us," Louise says. "Now that we're home, maybe he'll come back." Tears tumble down her little cheeks and my mum wipes them away.

"No," she says. "He won't."

"Is it because we went away and left him?" Louise asks, and stares up at my mum with pleading, wet eyes. I look at my mum. She can't look at me. She shakes her head.

"No," she says. "It wasn't that." Then something changes in her face, a shift in expression that is subtle, yet terrifying. Still smiling, she tells Louise to get the squeaky bone we got him and to put it on the doorstep, just in case he comes back.

Once she has left the kitchen, my mum looks at me with coldness in her eyes that I'll never forget. "You're old enough to know what happened," she says. "But Louise can't know. You had better not repeat what I'm about to tell you, because if you do, so help me I'll…"

I nod, cowering from her raised hand. My throat is dry and I feel tears well in my eyes. "I won't."

She straightens. "Your dad and I took him to the vet."

"Was he poorly?"

"No."

"Then what did you take him to the vet's for? Is he still there?"

She clears her throat. "We took him to the vet to get him put down. He was destroying everything and he kept running away. He ruined my good shoes, he chewed through the cable of the alarm clock making your dad late for work, and he dug up all the roses in the front garden. We just lost patience with him."

Between sobs, Louise shouts his name into the street from the open doorway.

"You killed my dog?" I ask, my voice barely a whisper.

She smiles at me, but there's no warmth behind it. Her eyes are lifeless. Her head nods.

"But I loved him."

She shrugs her shoulders and makes a noise that might be a laugh as she walks into the living room, leaving me on my own. "Then view this as a lesson in life." She turns to face me, saying one more thing before heading out into the garden to help Louise shout for him to come home. "Be very careful what you love," she says. "It will only leave you one day."

I am seven years old. My parents have killed my dog. And my mum, with one simple phrase, has shaped the rest of my life.

3

The street stretched out before her: a long, lonely tunnel that gradually faded into the inky black. Two rows of orange lights lined its path, distantly merging into one. She held her breath, held onto her charge even tighter. The boy-pirate screamed, but his fear fused with the others into one terrible noise. She wanted to shut her eyes again but couldn't. There was never as much pain if you shut your eyes, she told herself, just as her mother had once told her, but they remained open, staring straight ahead as if a way out of her situation waited at the end of the street, at the end of the tunnel of lights and all she had to do was see it. A miracle was what she needed. Maybe tonight one would offer itself to her.

She felt nothing at first. There was no pain, no sudden or violent agony as the car hit and her legs flew up before her. It was as though she had slipped on ice. The screams had stopped, she realised, and an empty silence surrounded her. The tunnel vanished from view, taking any hope of salvation with it, and it was replaced by the eternal black sky. She saw the stars, tried to count them. So many, she thought as her breath left her lungs in a massive surge. Instinctively, her grip around the boy-pirate tightened. She heard a crack quickly followed by another. They may have been feelings, rather than sounds – she couldn't be sure – and then suddenly she was catapulted forward.

Her world spun like she was on the scariest of all roller-coasters, but she knew only one thing mattered: she must keep her eyes to the sky; she must not let the boy-pirate hit the road first. She looked for the stars, for the tiny pricks of light that would hopefully save his young life, but everything was a blur. She tried to breathe, but nothing happened. She heard a snap, then another, then another and felt her grip loosen. She knew she was still moving, but she had lost all sense of direction. And then, at last, she saw them: dozens of stars, maybe hundreds, maybe thousands, sparkling silver and blue and white as they lit up the night sky above her. She was sliding on her back, she realised, and the view was wonderful. Why had she never seen stars like those before?

Another crack, only this time she felt the motion cease. Again, she tried to breathe, but couldn't. She held the boy-pirate, his weight still pressing down on her, his young body shielded from the concrete by her own. Now, her world was still; now her world was silent. And as her eyes slowly slid shut, she wondered if she'd saved him.

Chapter Three

Today is Thursday. Today is my birthday. Today, I am twenty-three years old.

I open my eyes to the pale light of early morning as it slides through the gap in the curtains. Memories of last night play in my mind like a favourite old movie, and I find myself smiling. The girls and I out on the town; Italian food and French wine; crazy dancing and even crazier cocktails; Louise (who drinks far too much for my liking) trying to convince the very gorgeous waiter to marry her; and drunken conversations with strangers as we wait for taxis to take us home. My senses waken as I stretch and yawn. I wait for a few seconds for the familiar signs of a hangover to reveal themselves, and then I relax. My head feels slightly tender, but with some breakfast and painkillers, I'll be fine.

I roll over and stare at the pillow. Empty. I imagine, as I do every morning, waking up with him watching me sleep. I wonder again at the point of me even having a double bed. I think of my little sister, of how effortlessly she can pick up men and put them back down again where she found them, both parties glad for their time together. I think of all my lost and wasted opportunities, but I quickly shake the thought from my mind. I am not my sister, and she is not me. Besides, the girls love watching guys flirt with me; they all know how it will end. Louise gave me a nickname a few years ago, and it's stuck to me like glue ever since. Although it's playful and not malicious in any way, I have to admit it's an accurate depiction of my attitude towards men in general.

They call me "Ice Queen".

I run my hand across the pillow. The feel is cool and crisp and clean. I'm beginning to forget what it's like to open my eyes to someone's smile, to run my fingers through tousled hair, or to rest my head on their shoulder as they lay sleeping. It's been so very, very long. The smile still sits on my lips, but it's a sad one now. I ask myself why anyone would want to be with me, especially now, especially with the news I expect to receive. I close my eyes. Thoughts of today, thoughts of the hospital, thoughts I have fought so hard to keep down begin to surface and I move quickly to dispel them. Positive thinking: that's what the nurses and doctors have told me to use, but it's easier said than done. Positive thinking: that's why we all went out last night, to chase away any lingering worries. Positive thinking: two simple words that project images of an imagined, hazy future; but one that's unreal to me.

I turn to lie on my back and take deep, calming breaths, staring at strips of morning's amber and gold across the white ceiling. Tiny curls of dust dance and swirl. Soft waves of lavender pass over me. I sink further into the mattress. My hands rest on my belly. Gently, I press down, whispering silent prayers to no God in particular, sending what little hope I have left into my uncertain insides. I decide, at that moment, I need my baby sister with me today.

The fluorescent green LED on the alarm clock tells me that it is not yet nine. I take only a moment to decide, and then I pick up the receiver to call her. It's a male voice that answers, and I hear a brief struggle – a moment of discomfort in the background – before she comes to the phone. She hears the nerves in my voice right away and agrees to meet me at the hospital. I ask if the waiter was worth the wait. She laughs, and says "God, yes," then cuts the connection.

I roll my eyes, smiling as I put the phone down. My sister: I love her so very, very, much.

~

The room is on the third floor of the newest part of the hospital. Millions have been spent modernising the building, making it feel less like an institution and more like a hotel. The walls are clean and white, dressed with colourful paintings and photographs of sunsets and beaches. The tiled floors gleam, and the furniture is modern and comfortable. Everything is there for a purpose. Everything is there to make you relax. Everything is there to help you forget the reason you are here.

Louise and I ride the elevator in a silence neither comfortable nor awkward; it just feels right not to say anything. Quiet piano music plays from a speaker above the control panel; rich, burgundy carpets climb knee-high up the walls; spotless, silver mirrors sparkle in the soft ambient light. I watch my sister. The elevator is perfect and I can tell she wants to put her hands onto the glass, leaving her mark, creating just a little bit of disorder. But she is on her best behaviour today. She is even biting her bottom lip with the effort of restraint.

"That must have been difficult for you, sis," I say as we walk along the corridor towards the offices. She looks at me and grins.

"You have no idea," she says and takes my arm in hers.

We wait on deep-filled faux-leather chairs for only a few minutes before my name is called. Louise offers to wait where she is, but I want her with me. Either way, good news or bad, I need my best friend by my side. She slides her hand into mine and kisses me on the cheek. Together, we enter the office

4

Muffled voices struggled to make sense to her; warm fingers pressed against her neck. She felt the cold of the tarmac seep through her jeans, numbing her legs. Her body was heavy – too heavy to move. Her arms, like solid lead, rested by her side and her eyes seemed to sink deeper into her skull with every passing moment. But something wasn't right, she knew. It was as though a tremendous weight sat on her chest, making her unable to breathe. Muffled voices, heavy eyes – all she wanted to do was fall asleep. She tried to roll over onto her side, but the weight pinned her to the ground. Cold jeans or wet jeans – did it matter? Again, voices, only this time not so vague. They were talking to her, she realised, telling her to do something, quickly, urgently, now. She had to focus, to force herself to listen to the voices. She shut her eyes harder, felt them fall further into their sockets as she did so. Then the soft tendrils of a woman's voice reached her, her words melting through the fog.

"Breathe," the voice said. "Breathe."

Chapter Four

After years of being teased about it by other children, my ginger hair has finally begun to darken, light chestnut roots showing the colour my hair will eventually become. I wear braces on my teeth, two strips of shiny metal that make me even more self-conscious than I already am. I've taken a growth spurt recently; I'm nearly taller than my mum. A few spots have visited my forehead in recent weeks, small red lumps on oily skin, and I'm starting to get hair on places I've never had hair before. A few nights ago, when my aunt was visiting, she sat with me in my room and told me how my body would develop over the next few years. Even though I knew most of it already, it felt great to be told these things by someone who knows for sure. Maybe it should have been my mum, but she and I will never be friends – not like my aunt and I are. During our chat, she told me about periods, warned me about boys and gave me loads of make-up tips. Then, smiling playfully as she looked at my chest, she suggested it was time I got my first bra.

So today, Saturday, my aunt, uncle and I are going shopping. Mum says it's up to me whether or not Louise is allowed to go, and I look at her as she stands at the door, smiling hopefully, clinging to my old stripy-pyjama panda that never leaves her side, and I say it's ok: she can come. Even though today is meant to be about me, she is my sister and I love her with all my heart.

We eat lunch in Louise's favourite burger place. I have the chicken, because that's what my aunt orders. My sister eats like she hasn't had food for days, devouring her own meal, most of mine, my uncle's fries and then an ice-cream for dessert. I wonder where she puts it all, she's so thin. She says she has to feed her panda, and makes a pitiful attempt at giving him a drink from her straw. We all laugh. Her eyes are big and shiny and powder-blue, and she smiles as though butter wouldn't melt in her mouth; it's hard not to believe her when she looks so beautiful.

We head into the mall. The stores on the main street are great for clothes shopping, but my aunt says she wants to take me to a specialist underwear shop. She also tells me she's paying for my bra, so I don't argue. For the first time in my life, I feel like an adult.

My uncle wants to go and look at the televisions, or so he says. I notice the smirk on my aunt's face as she kisses him goodbye, and she looks at me. "Men," is all she says; I think I understand what she means.

I love spending proper grown-up time with my aunt. The lady in the store gives me loads of advice about being measured regularly and about wearing the correct type of bra for the occasion. Not only does my aunt buy me three bras – one black, two white – but she gets me loads of new underwear, too. She said only I can decide which cut is the most comfortable for me to wear, so I leave the shop with two pairs of every kind. She is like my big sister and my best friend rolled into one. I wish my mum could be more like her.

On the hour, we head back to the mall-front, where we arranged to meet up with my uncle. I feel so different with my bra on, carrying a bag filled with proper grown-up underwear, walking with my arm in my aunts, like I was sixteen. I have the neck of my t-shirt pulled as far to one side as I can, showing the white cotton strap on my shoulder. I decide that from today even though I'm only eleven, I will try to act more like an adult. I decide that today is one of the best days of my life.

We see him at the entrance, and he smiles and waves as we approach.

"Look at you," he says to me, pointing to the bra-strap, and I blush.

"She's a young woman now," my aunt says to him, and I beam with joy that she thinks the same as I do. I feel like I've been accepted into some secret club.

I give her a kiss on the cheek and she puts her arm around my shoulder and squeezes me into her.

"Shall we head home?" she asks, and smiling, happy, the three of us make for the doors.

My uncle stops and looks around himself. "Where's Louise?" I realise she is nowhere to be seen.

"She was with you," my aunt says, and when I see the look on his face, my stomach turns to stone.

"No, she stayed with you guys. I haven't seen her since I left you upstairs."

My blood runs cold. My sister: where is she?

During that summer, two little boys from my school had gone missing. The police searched everywhere for them, knocking on every door and speaking to almost every single person in the town. There were photos on bus stops and lamp posts – *Have You Seen These Boys?* – and their faces were shown on the news every night. A newspaper offered a reward to anyone who gave information that led to them being found. Everything possible was done to find them. Everything was done to bring them home safe.

After three weeks, the news reported that two bodies had been found alongside the railway tracks. My mum had to explain to me what a shallow grave was. They never caught the person who did it. The boys were dead and the murderer was still at large.

And now, my baby sister is missing.

Panic sets in. Something I haven't felt before grips my throat and won't let go. I start to cry. It's completely irrational, I know; my uncle is perfectly calm; my aunt puts her arm around my shoulders; some people look at me with concern as they pass.

"I'll head back up to the television section," he says. "Maybe she's watching a movie or something." He winks at me and strokes my damp cheek before he disappears into the crowd.

I wait with my aunt. She wants to go back up to the lingerie store, but I tell her to wait on my uncle coming back. She starts to suggest leaving me here to wait on him while she goes and looks, but she stops when she sees the look of terror on my face. Instead, she holds me and I sob into her collar.

A security lady comes up to us and asks if we're okay. My aunt explains what's happening. The security lady pats me on the shoulder. "It happens all the time," she says. I think it's meant to make me feel better. It doesn't. She mumbles a description of Louise into her radio. "The control room can check the entire mall on the cameras for her," she says.

I nod. Thoughts of those two little boys…

My shoulders shake as pain gathers in the pit of my stomach, manifesting itself as a moan I cannot stop. My aunt holds me tighter. I hear passers-by stop to make sure I'm okay. I lift my head from her shoulder, seeing nothing through the haze of tears. My breath catches in my throat and I choke, coughing noisily into my hands. I feel my bra cut into my shoulders and around my chest, but nothing else matters. We have to find Louise.

I hear a voice behind me: my uncle. I turn, and in less than half a second before I see him, I feel hope, expectation, joy, fear, sorrow, trepidation and sadness.

I wipe my damp eyes. He looks at me, but his face is expressionless.

He is alone.

A crowd has gathered, most of them looking at me. A whisper of concern passes from one mouth to the next. I hear the words "lost" and "shame" and "those two little boys". There is a crackle of static, and the security lady holds her radio to her ear. She smiles, sadly. "They are still looking," she says, and she pats my arm reminding me not to worry.

"I thought she was with you guys," my uncle says to no one in particular. "I thought she was with you" and he clasps his fingers together behind his head, looking at the distant sky through the glass ceiling. He takes in several slow, deep breaths.

"What was she wearing?" a voice from the crowd asks. "What age is she?" asks another. My aunt answers. "Did she have any bags with her?"

I lift my head and wipe my eyes. She didn't have any bags with her, but she did have her stripy-pyjama panda. Hope runs through me. I grab my aunt's hand and drag her towards the escalator. I know where she is.

Within a few steps, I let go of her hand and run. My heart races, beating in time with my legs as one store after another blurs past me. I hear nothing but the voice in my head, telling me she will be safe, urging me to hurry. I imagine what I will do when I see her. I picture rushing up to her, where we hug each other and she thanks me for coming to find her and I tell her I love her and she says the same to me. In my mind, it's like the movies; there's even music playing in the background.

I reach the Make-A-Bear store first, barely ahead of my uncle, who has realised where she is, too. I stop at the entrance as I catch sight of her, sitting cross-legged on the wooden floor playing with my old stripy-pyjama panda. Outfits and accessories are randomly scattered around her. She doesn't look up. It's then I realise she won't know we've been looking for her.

I hear my uncle sigh with relief as he sees her, and I feel the weight of the world release from his shoulders. He signals two thumbs-up to my aunt, who slows to a stop and hides her face in her hands. Then he whistles and Louise looks up, smiling as she sees us both. She stands up, and I walk over to her. Recent thoughts of never seeing her again fill my mind, and I feel the tingle of tears at the back of my nose. I think of all the things I want to say to her. I want to tell her to never leave me. I want to hold her and never let me go.

"Hey, sis," she says as she swings her panda by the arm as she comes to the front of the store. My aunt is with us now, and she sits her hand on my shoulder. Thoughts of reunion, cinematic music, and words we will both remember forever churn through my mind. She is within arm's-length. I reach out to her with my left hand and she takes it in hers.

Then I slap her.

I slap her hard across her face. The sound is sharp, like the crack of a whip. Strangers turn to see what the noise was. My hand stings immediately. There is a stunned silence that follows, before anyone can react, before my sister even realises what has just happened.

"Don't you ever do that to me again!" I hiss at her through clenched teeth. "Ever! Do you hear me?"

Her face contorts as she screams in pain. My uncle is between us in a flash and scoops her up in his arms.

My aunt spins me round and wears a look I have never seen on her before: Horror; revulsion; disgust. Realisation sears through me. All my thoughts of sentiment have deserted me; any notion of affection, abandoned. I stare wide-eyed and open-mouthed, repulsed by what I have done. I cover my mouth with my burning palm.

"I'm sorry," I whisper as I shake my head. "Louise, I'm so sorry." I want to reach out to her, but I'm frozen.

I am eleven years old. I think of my mother, of the times where she has shown me nothing but pain instead of love, of all the years she has seemingly taken pride in hurting me, and I realise I have become her.

In that instant, my life changes; I swear I will never let her poison me again.

5

Suddenly, it was clear what was wrong. There was no great weight pressing down on her chest, there was nothing pinning her to the ground. She needed to breathe; her body starved of the oxygen it required was slowly shutting down. The voices she could hear were telling her to stay alive.

She thought of him then, of her reason to live. Tonight's dinner was ruined, but surely there would be others. He would understand – at least she hoped he would. He was considerate about things like tonight. He would see what she had done, and he would not be upset or angry. He was a good man; she was lucky to have him. Yes, she thought, he would understand. She imagined her future, their future, the pictures of the life they would share together pulsing in her mind like a strobe. And then she remembered the boy-pirate. Where was he? Was he safe? Did he get hurt? The pain in her chest was becoming unbearable now, the invisible weight growing heavier and heavier.

Breathe, she told herself. Breathe now.

She opened her mouth and with a loud inward gasp filled her burning lungs with as much air as they could take. Freezing cold spilled down her throat, and for a second or two, as her chest filled, she felt nothing but relief.

Then the pain started: A few tiny needle-pricks at first, mainly in her stomach, followed closely by more and soon more again, spreading throughout her body as though a swarm of bees all stung at once. From her stomach, it went to her legs and chest; her arms *were next, then her feet and hands. Finally, it reached her head, and it felt like nothing she had endured before. Her eyes rolled and she tried to arch her back as the pain swelled, but she couldn't move. She heard a scream – a shrill, terror-filled wail that pierced right through skin and bone – and realised it had come from her lips. Mouth agape, she opened her eyes wide to the stars.*

Chapter Five

My aunt and I are in her kitchen, preparing dinner. I'm meant to be helping, but she is so organised that I end up doing nothing more than washing each dish and utensil as she finishes with it. The sink is at the window, and I watch my sister work in the long back garden. A thick carpet of copper and gold covers the grass, and Louise, rake in hand, sweeps up the fallen leaves into an ever-growing pile. She breathes hard with her efforts, and the air leaves her in wisps of ice-blue. She wants to do it as a surprise for our uncle. She dotes on him, seizing every opportunity to be with him and do things that will make him like her more. Even though both my aunt and I told her she didn't have to do anything, that he loves her for who she is not what she does, she wanted to clear the back garden of leaves for him coming home. I wipe beads of condensation from the glass and smile as I look at her, innocent and child-like. But she is growing quickly – she was nine in the summer past – and even as wrapped-up against the cold as she is, her legs appear too long for her body. She sees me watching and excitedly waves a gloved hand. Big blue eyes beam out against rosy cheeks and a button nose, and she has a smile that could thaw ice. She is, without question, the most beautiful thing I have ever seen.

A buzzer sounds from the oven and my aunt opens the door to check on the pie. She mutters under her breath as she checks her watch, turns the temperature down and lets the door close with a thud. Raising one eye-brow, she shakes her head as she looks at me. "Men," is all she says. My face is a mirror of hers.

I open the window slightly to let some heat escape. The hem of the net curtain dances and the glass begins to clear. My aunt comes to stand with me. Together, we watch Louise drag her rake from the back of the garden to the front. She knows we are watching, but doesn't look up. It's only when the garden is cleared of most of the leaves, when the pile is at waist height that she stops and with a dramatic pose, says "look what I've done!"

"We'll see," my aunt says under her breath, and winks at me. She opens the door and heads outside. I grin. I can guess what's coming next.

I grab my coat from the back of the chair in the dining room and follow her out into the garden. Louise still stands proudly by her leaves.

"Good job, Lou," my aunt says. "But you missed some over there."

She points to a spot over Louise's shoulder, and as my sister turns to see, my aunt shouts "Now!" and we both begin showering her with handfuls of leaves. She squeals and runs up the garden as fast as her long legs can carry her. We give chase and within seconds my aunt has Louise on the ground.

"Save me!" she squeals between laughs, in the voice of her childhood. My aunt is sitting on my sister's chest, her knees pinning her arms to the grass. We begin stuffing fistfuls of leaves down her jacket. Louise is hysterical.

"It's freezing!" she shouts. "Please someone save me!"

My aunt is laughing so hard she struggles to catch breath. Tears of laughter run down my face and my cheeks hurt.

"Save me!"

I collapse on the ground beside my sister; I can hardly move. My aunt looks at me, and I shake my head.

"I'm done," I manage.

With a sigh, she rolls over to the other side of Louise.

The echo of joy floats unending on the chill air around us. I hold my sister's left hand, my aunt her right. The three of us lie on the cold grass, staring up at the clear night sky. A dusting of silver stars smile down on us, twinkling from thousands of years ago. We lay together without speaking, our breath the only sound. I give my sister's hand a little squeeze and I close my eyes.

I know I'll remember this moment for the rest of my life.

~

My uncle still isn't home.

The time for being late has come and gone, and now my aunt is worried. She serves up dinner for the three of us, keeping his plateful warm in the oven. She says nothing, but she doesn't have to – her eyes convey more emotion than words ever could.

We eat in heavy silence, the memory of our fun in the garden fading. Even Louise chews her food quietly, looking at me, then my aunt every few seconds. As I place my knife and fork beside each other on my gravy-streaked plate, I thank my aunt for dinner. Louise, as usual, is moments behind me, even though she has eaten almost twice as much food as I have. She burps loudly, and smiles. I stifle a laugh. My aunt doesn't appear to notice.

"I'll get dessert," I say and begin clearing the plates. My aunt follows me into the kitchen, leaving Louise on her own at the table.

"It's not like him not to have called," she says. There is worry in her voice. "Even if he was working late, or there was a delay on the trains or, well, anything..." Her voice trails off as she marches across the kitchen and picks up the phone. She holds it to her ear for no more than a second before replacing the receiver. "At least we know the phone is working."

As I spoon the desserts onto the plates, I begin to formulate a plan for Louise and I to disappear upstairs for a while when my uncle finally gets home. By the look on my aunt's face, he's in a lot of trouble and he'll be lucky to escape with his life; I don't want my sister around when she launches her pain at him. Louise joins us, the floorboards creaking as she treads carefully into the kitchen.

"Well," my aunt says to Louise. "It looks like you might be getting a second dinner tonight."

My little sister smiles and runs across to my aunt, wrapping her arms around her, holding tightly. It's clear we all feel the same: There is something in the air; something is definitely wrong.

"I'm sure he'll be fine," she whispers. My aunt kisses the top of her head.

"I hope so," is all she can manage.

Its two hours later before the doorbell rings.

The noise punctuates the stillness like a hammer and I jump with fright. We hesitate, no one moves, the three of us frozen together in time. It rings again. My sister and I look at each other, then my aunt. She wears a blank, empty face, but behind her eyes I know she is preparing herself for everything and for anything. It rings a third time. She stands, carefully smoothes down her blouse and leaves the room.

We hear voices from the front door. Louise heads to the window and lifts the curtain aside to see who is there. She gasps. Quickly I move to her side and look out into the night. I lift my hand to my mouth. Cold settles into the pit of my stomach. My sister looks at me. Tears spring to my eyes.

It's the police.

~

We buried him this morning, six days after the accident.

It's a bright sunny day, windless, not a cloud in the sky. I'm outside the pub where everyone from the service is eating a lunch of soup and sandwiches, laid on by my aunt. She is inside, keeping herself busy, not allowing herself any time for reflection. She says she has the rest of her life to do that.

I'm on my own, wrapped up warm against the chill, taking tiny bites from a cheese sandwich. I stare at the empty trees, black shadows against the crystal-blue backdrop. Thoughts of my uncle chase the memories of him around my head. I still can't get used to the notion of never seeing him again. Louise is in pieces. She won't stop crying, and seems to have enough tears for all of us. My mum, to her credit, has been wonderful with my aunt, knowing when to help, when to back down, and when to take over in regard to organising the funeral, dealing with insurance companies, and the like. But I have found peace in the quiet things. I draw a little bit of solace from being in my own company, letting my thoughts run their course.

A bird lands on the grass in front of me. I throw it some chunks of bread from the sandwich I can no longer face eating. It hops over to one of the pieces and swallows it whole. Then it takes another in its beak and lifts skyward, disappearing into the distant trees.

There is nothing here now. No movement, no sound. I am completely alone. I try to remember the last time we were together, just my uncle and me, and I can't. Either Louise or my aunt was always with us. I try to remember the last time he cuddled me, tickling my ribs to make me laugh and squirm the way he had done all my life, but the memories are foggy. And I try to remember the last time I told him I loved him.

The door opens behind me. Louise steps up to stand with me, saying nothing, watching her breath melt into the air. Arms folded, she rests her head on my shoulder and I slide my arm round her back. Her eyes are pink holes on charcoal, her cheeks drawn, and her skin pale and dry. She is disappearing into herself, drowning in grief, and I don't know how to stop her. I hold her tighter.

"It's so unfair," she whispers. "Why did he have to die?"

I kiss her hair, and my silence answers her question.

"She's in there just now," she continues, "our aunt, all alone now, and she looks so sad. I can't believe none of us will ever see him again. I miss him so…" The words catch in her throat as her tears fall once more.

I fill my lungs with bitter-cold air. "He's with us in our hearts and our memories, isn't he?" She nods once and sniffs. "And we need to be strong for our aunt, now, don't we? And we need to be there for our mum and for each other, too?" She nods again. I stare into the low white sun, thinking of the past, imagining the future, and wondering what to say next to make my baby sister feel better.

"When I'm older," Louise says, her voice low, "when I fall in love like in the fairy-stories, if anything happened to my husband, I wouldn't want to be without him; I wouldn't want to be like our aunt. I'd make sure we were together forever."

My arms squeeze her closer. "There are some things you can't control, Louise," I say. "Do you think our aunt wanted him to die?" She shakes her head and coughs gently. "But there's always hope, you know? Even when it all seems pointless, we have to believe that tomorrow, it will be better. And maybe, just maybe, things won't end the way we think."

She looks up at me with glassy eyes, kisses my cheek and forces a smile. Then she slides her fingers round mine and leads me back into the pub into the waiting arms of my aunt.

6

Voices spoke to her in calming tones, hushing her as they would a baby. One voice, almost certainly female, reached into her more than the others.

"Try not to move," it whispered. She felt a hand rest on her forehead. "An ambulance is on the way."

Her vision was blurred; the skin on her face felt raw and open. Gently, the stranger's fingers brushed at her cheeks, wiping the icy tears away. Immediately, her face felt better. There was a wheezing, followed by a gargling sound and with each of the latter, fingers feathered at the corners of her mouth. It took her a moment to realise the noises were of her own breath; it was another minute or so, once the metallic taste took hold, before she understood the fingers were removing thin tracers of blood from her lips.

She was cold. Waves of excruciating pain surged through her body constantly, yet a growing numbness fought each onslaught with silent relief. She stopped screaming almost immediately after she started; the pain in her lungs shortening her breath to a point where speech was almost impossible. Still the voice spoke to her, soft and soothing, gently reassuring her she would be all right. She stared at the star-filled sky, unable to see them through her watery haze. A face appeared, blurred, unrecognisable, but she knew it was a face. She tried to focus on it, willing it closer. Her lungs felt heavy, her throat tight. She took the biggest breath she could. *The pain nearly made her pass out, but she stayed alert; she just had to know.*

"The pirate," she murmured, her voice sounding to her like air passing through water. "The boy – did I save him?"

Chapter Six

It is the night of my first high school Christmas dance.

I'm sitting on a chair in my aunt's dining room with a towel wrapped round me. She is styling my hair, wrapping it in over-sized rollers to make big, bouncy curls, chatting away to me like I'm a client at her work – but I'm not really paying attention to what she is saying; my mind is on tonight. I picture my dress – it's hanging on the back of her bedroom door – and I look at the several pairs of shoes my aunt has sat out for me to choose from, trying to imagine which pair goes best. I chew on my thumbnail. Excitement makes my knees spring up and down and my aunt wraps her hands around my throat, laughing as she tells me to sit still for the hundredth time.

"Stop worrying about tonight!" she says, and kisses my cheek. "You'll look absolutely beautiful. Here, I know you're still a few years from it being legal, but I bought us this."

She goes to the fridge, takes out a bottle of wine and fills two glasses. A crisp, pale-yellow Chardonnay that tastes of melon trickles down my throat, cold and refreshing. The hairdryer whirrs to life, and she continues to work on my hair. I let the heat wash over me and try to calm down. I love the way my aunt talks to me and treats me like an adult, even though I'm not. It's far more than I can say about my mum.

I glance at the clock above the door. He should be here to

pick me up in an hour. I take another sip of wine, and feel my knees begin to twitch again.

"Are you nervous because of him?" she asks, switching the hairdryer off and coming round to face me. I nod. She's referring to my date. "Well, from what you've told me about him, he sounds like a really nice boy. And if that is the case, all you need to be is yourself – nothing more, nothing less. He will like you for who you are."

I smile self-consciously. I know she's right. But I also know that tonight is my first ever date, and I have never been kissed before, not properly anyway. I hope it happens tonight; I hope it's with him.

She pats me on my bare knees and then finishes my hair as I dream of the next few hours.

Up in her bedroom, she applies my make-up. I'm halfway through my second glass of wine, which combined with the nerves and excitement I feel for tonight, is making me light-headed. I sway slightly as she colours my eyelids.

"I remember the first time I kissed someone," she says, as though she has been reading my mind the entire night. I look at her and I feel my cheeks flush. "He was seventeen, a whole two years older than me; I was your age. It was after a group of us went to the cinema and he offered to walk me home." She smiles, lost in her thoughts and memories. I sit perfectly still, and listen; she hardly ever talks about the past. "It was a summers' night, not a breath of wind, the smell of cut grass and barbecues everywhere. Even though it was warm, I had a jacket with me, and I carried it over my arms as we walked. He asked me if he could carry it for me, and when I asked him why he wanted to do that, he said it was because he wanted to hold my hand." She pauses, then, staring at a space over my shoulder.

"And did you let him?" I ask.

"I laughed at him," she says, smiling, her eyes still finding something in the distance. "We were friends, nothing more, and not even good friends at that. I had never looked at him as anything other than the quiet boy who knew my older brother. But you know what? As we walked the rest of the way home, as we both realised we knew so little about one another, the idea of him being more than a friend stopped being so alien to me. Sure, he wasn't the most handsome boy in school; he wasn't into sports or anything like the rest of the guys – but he was interesting, you know? And funny; he made me laugh so hard that night! He was... well... different. We had lots in common, which was a surprise to me, too. So as we turned into my street, I asked him if his offer to carry my jacket was still open."

The smile on my face must have reached from one ear to the other. I have never heard her speak like this before. "You're nothing but an old romantic!" I say. She grins.

"And when he slid his hand into mine, I felt something raw, something powerful that ripped the breath from my lungs. I hadn't known anything like it in my life! I remember looking at him, and seeing in his eyes that he felt the same thing. I didn't think, at that moment, I could have released his hand, even if I wanted to. It was something special, it really was."

"And did he kiss you right there and then?"

"No," she says, barely shaking her head. "The walk along my street seemed to last forever; neither of us wanted it to end. The sun had set, but it wasn't dark; the sky was still a 'thousand blue', and the way my heart was beating, I wouldn't have felt any chill in the air anyway. We finally got to my front door. My parents were in the living room watching television, but the curtains were drawn. We stood with my back against the heavy wooden door and just looked into each other's eyes, our faces inches apart, and our breaths shallow and synchronised. He lifted up his hand to touch my cheek, and…" She stops talking. There are tears in her eyes now, and a look of loss on her face. The edges of her pink, glossy lips are raised in a sad smile.

"And what?" I ask. "What happened next?"

She sighs, and then returns from her memory by raising her eyebrows. She blinks her tears away.

"Well," she says with happiness in her voice, "It turned out he was an absolutely terrible kisser! I didn't know what I was expecting, but it certainly wasn't what I got." She laughs and dusts my cheeks light pink. "But it worked out all right in the end. We taught one another how to get better, and over the years, he ended up being rather good at it."

I look at her. My forehead creases as her words sink in. "Do you mean he was…"

My aunt smiles, her perfect white teeth shining. "Yes," she says. "The boy I kissed that night – the only boy I have ever kissed – turned out to be your uncle."

She finishes my make-up and goes downstairs to make some tea for herself. I put my underwear on in silence, her story running through my head, joining with my imagination. I wonder what I would do if I knew for a fact that the boy I kiss tonight (hopefully) would be the only one ever. Would I postpone it to get some experience? Would I run a mile at the thought of never being able to kiss another? Or would I embrace the notion? It worked out for my aunt and uncle. Why would it not work out for me, too?

I catch myself dreaming and curse silently. Knowing my luck, he'll probably not even turn up and I'll be forced to dance with the guys who couldn't get a date. The thought makes me shudder.

I remove the dress from the hanger, and step into it. It's as light as a feather; the feel of silk on my skin is luxurious. There is a full-length mirror in the corner of the room, and as I stand before it, I gasp. The image of myself I've known my whole life has aged in the last few hours, unrecognisable from before; the girl becomes the woman; the ugly duckling, the swan. With delicate fingers, my reflection smoothes down the edges of the fabric where it ends below the knee-line and stands straight once more. I smile at her and she smiles back. My aunt has done a wonderful job with my hair and make-up. Even if I do say so myself, I think I look quite pretty tonight.

I open the door and go to the top of the stairs. There is a pair of shoes waiting for me, ones I have not seen before. They are silver, with little purple stones the same colour as my dress, and a handbag to match. As I slip the shoes on, I take a deep breath and smile with gratitude. She has taken care of everything for me.

"Well," I shout down to her. "What do you think?"

She comes to the bottom of the stairs, looks up at me and claps her hands, glowing with joy. "You look so beautiful!" she cries, and beckons me down. She hugs me and I hug her back. "I can't believe you're the same little girl I've watched grow up! There will be no one as gorgeous as you there tonight, let me tell you."

I start to correct her, because I know there will be lots of girls there who are far prettier than me, but she hushes me quickly.

"I wish he could see you," she says, and a familiar, dull ache passes through me like a ghost tiptoeing on my soul. Even though it's been almost two and a half years since he died, the wound still feels open. I have no words to respond; all I can do is hug her once more.

We stand like that for a few long moments, emotion threatening to overwhelm us both, when the doorbell rings. It's him. He's here. She skips to the door, wiping her eyes, leaving me at the foot of the stairs, petrified. "Are you ready?" I shake my head. "Too late!" she says, and opens the door wide.

~

That night, I danced only with Robert. My nerves dissolved completely as we held one another for the first dance, and now, at the end of the night, with only a few tunes left, it's like we've been joined together forever.

I close my eyes, hardly able to believe how well the evening has gone. The dozen red roses he bought me will be, by now, in a vase in my aunt's kitchen. Midway through the evening, he asked the band to play my favourite song and he whispered the lyrics in my ear as we swayed in time to the music. Now it's a couples-only dance; we are one of just three pairs on the floor.

I rest my head on his shoulder, my arms around his back, my fingers spread wide to hold as much of him as possible. He smells wonderful. The music wraps us in swathes of peace and comfort. I imagine we are the only two people in the whole world. I feel his mouth touch my ear, his warm breath sending a shiver down the length of my body. "Would you like to go outside for a while?" he whispers. Without looking up, I nod.

He leads me out into the calm December night. We walk, hand in hand, on the long tree-lined gravel driveway that leads from the hotel venue to the road. For a few moments, neither of us speaks. The sound of the band has faded into the distance. Thoughts of our friends inside have vanished. As we near the road, the maze of bare branches above us ends, revealing a cloudless, starry sky. I look up and I smile.

"A thousand blue," I say, and within a few more steps, I stop walking.

"What does that mean?" he asks.

"It doesn't really mean anything. It was something my aunt said earlier on tonight."

He grins, and comes to stand in front of me, the gap

between us mere inches. "I like your nose," he says and rests his finger on it.

"I broke it when I was little and it didn't set properly. That's why it's so squinty." For the first time, I'm not embarrassed about it – no one has ever said they like it before.

Over his shoulder, the full moon sails across the sky, a perfect circle of pure, glacier white. Silence whispers from the shadows. There is not a hint of wind and tomorrow morning's frost is already crisp in the air. I can't imagine a more perfect setting.

I lift my fingers to his cheek. I'm shaking, but not with the cold. His hands rest on the small of my back. I close my eyes, and open my mouth slightly. My lips are dry. He leans forward; I breathe him in. My heart pounds in my ears. An army of jumbled thoughts scurry through my mind, screaming in silence. Our lips finally touch for the first time; wave after wave of strange feelings ripple through me, feelings of indescribable happiness and joy.

And as we kiss, I know this moment is mine forever.

7

The echo of two-tone sirens punctuated the frigid night sky, adding to the growing sense of urgency shared by the growing crowd, huddled around the broken girl. Their number had swelled rapidly and now more than twenty onlookers jostled for space, trying to catch a glimpse of her. The vehicle, a dark-coloured family saloon, still had its engine running from beneath a dented bonnet, the exhaust breathing out silver plumes of smoke. The headlights still burned, allowing the crowd to see the scene, and the full extent of her injuries.

From the initial impact, she was lifted and carried by the car, then catapulted forward as it stopped. In total, she travelled more than forty feet, landing on her back and sliding before crunching to a halt against the wheels of a parked van. The icy conditions of the road meant she skidded further than she normally would have; it also meant she was able to remain on her back, protecting the boy-pirate from harm. There was a concerned whisper amongst the crowd; a constant drone that voiced the worried expressions on each of their faces. As one, they knew the situation was not good; they knew the injuries were serious.

Kneeling by her side, the woman who had told her not to move continued to reassure with gentle sounds and touch. Another voice joined hers, deeper, yet more calming. It reminded her of her uncle's voice whenever she hurt herself as a child; it wrapped her in comfort and safety – nothing bad would happen to her as long as he was with her. She closed her eyes against the pain, against the memory, and wished he were here with her now.

"I need you to be still," the male voice said. Soft fingers brushed cold tears from her face. The sound of sirens grew louder, more urgent. The buzz of the crowd she could not see was absorbed by the ambulance's approach and soon all she could hear was the shrill two-tone.

Then there was silence.

Chapter Seven

I open my eyes, barely aware I have slept. Complete darkness engulfs me. I strain my ears, listening as hard as I can for any sounds from the living room, from the hallway, or even from outside, but a heavy silence is all there is. I wonder what time it is, how much longer I have to wait here before I can get up. I think about my sister; she should still be asleep, but maybe I should check on her anyway – maybe I could persuade *her* to go and see if he's been. I let the notion brew in my thoughts for a few seconds, but I decide against it. I wouldn't want her to get nothing because of me. I try closing my eyes, urging my dreams to return, but I know I won't be able to get back to sleep now; excitement fills me to the point where I'm shivering. I lie like this for a long time, in the dark, in the quiet, and let the possibilities grow in my imagination.

When finally I can't wait any longer, breathing as quietly as I can, I slide from my bed and tiptoe to my door. Ben lifts his head from his basket at the foot of my bed, and I whisper for him to stay. He opens his jaw wide in a yawn, and then lays his head back between his paws. Slowly, I turn the handle and inch the door open. It drags on the carpet, and I bite my tongue, trying desperately not make any noise at all. When I can squeeze through the gap, I crawl along the hall and then creep down the stairs. The living room is directly in front of me; the door is closed over but not quite shut. With my ear against the wood, I listen for any movement from inside, and after a few seconds, satisfied there is no one there, I gently shove the door open.

The curtains are open and orange light from the streetlights outside floods the living room. Soundlessly, I stand up and close the door behind me. As my eyes adjust to the light, I open my mouth wide and clamp my hand over it quickly; it's all I can do not to yell out with joy: He's been!

Santa has been!

I look at the array of presents before me: On one side of the couch, mine; on the other, Louise's. My eyes take in everything he has left for me at once. The "Baby Sophie" dolls pram I asked for is there, as is the playpen, and a collection of outfits for her are fanned out between books, board games, sweets and chocolates. I have no idea what to pick up first, and the adrenalin coursing through my veins threatens to explode from my mouth in a squeal of sheer delight.

I take a small step backwards, calming myself, knowing I cannot make any noise. If my parents hear me, they'll tell me to go back to bed to wait until my sister wakens up, and that could be ages. I close my eyes and take slow, deep breaths, like my school teacher told us to do when we need to relax.

When I open them once more, I feel much better. I look around the living room. The tree sits like a huge shadow in the corner, the tinsel and baubles barely visible in the dim light, our carefully-wrapped presents for each other piled under it; five stockings hang from the fire-place, bulging with extra presents Santa left us on his way back up the chimney; the glass of milk we left for him is empty, and I smile proudly as I realise that the carrots I left out for his reindeer are all away. I tell myself it's because I washed them, certain the other girls in my class would not have been so considerate. I look again at my presents. I tried to be a good girl this year. It seems my efforts have been worth it.

And then I realise something: I cannot open any of my

things. My mum and dad would be really angry if they knew I was up before Louise. They even reminded us last night not to get up until they said so, just in case Santa hadn't been yet. The sense of joy I felt moments ago evaporates. I sigh and fold my skinny arms across my chest. I should go back to bed and wait on everyone. I look at the little carriage clock on the fireplace, squinting my eyes to make sense of the shadowy hands. It's only quarter past four. Disappointment smothers me; they won't be up for at least another two hours. The thought of wakening Louise edges to the front of my mind. If both of us were to get up, mum and dad would *have* to let us open our presents. Then they could go back to bed if they wanted to, and we could play all morning, until it was time to get ready for dinner. I look at the clock again and shake my head in frustration; I know it's far too early for everyone to get up.

I trudge across to the presents Santa has left for me. Even in the half-light, everything looks so shiny, so new. The temptation to open just one thing is almost too much, and I have to sit cross-legged on the floor, my hands clamped under me to resist.

I glance across at what he left for Louise. My brow furrows. She got "Baby Sophie" clothes too, but she got the rocking-horse and the laundry set. She only asked for them because I did first, but mum told me I could only get two things. I look at my pram and my play-pen. I've already got a pram for my dolls, and I wonder what fun there will be in playing with a play-pen. I wish I had asked for the horsey and the washing machine. And then I look at the clothes Santa left for her dolls and compare them to mine. She has far nicer things than I do. She has a wedding dress and a princess gown and an outfit that makes Sophie look like a pussycat. I have a nurse's uniform, a fairy costume and a swimsuit. I puff my cheeks out and groan. There's no way she has been better behaved than I have this year, no way at all.

A thought occurs to me then, something devious and sly. I

think of the fox in the stories my aunt reads to me, or the wolf. I picture Louise in her bed, on her side, wrapped up snugly in her blankets with her thumb in her mouth, and dreaming dreams of Santa and reindeer and snow. I love her with all my heart. Can I really be so selfish? Then I remember that no one knows what Santa has left for us, other than Santa, and he'll still be out there delivering presents. And he won't know, because mum won't know I've swapped presents, so she won't phone him. I grin from ear to ear. My plan is flawless.

As quietly as I can, I begin switching presents from one side of the couch to the other. It seems to take forever. My heart races and my hands tremble as I stand back and look at what I have done.

On my side, I now have the horse and the washing machine as well as the pram; Louise has the play-pen. And she is left with the nurse's uniform and the swimsuit; I have the four outfits I want. I bounce up and down on my toes, satisfaction and greed flowing through me in equal measures. Unable to resist I keep going, swapping games and other toys and chocolates around until my load of presents far outweighs hers. I console myself with the fact she is only four; I'm older, and I should get more things than her. I check the time. It's almost five o'clock. I clap my hands together quietly, proud of myself, and even prouder of my plan.

With one last look over my shoulder, I silently return to my room, slide under my covers and drift back to sleep.

~

Four hours later, and my world is in tatters.

I have been dragged into the kitchen by my mum, and she slams the door shut behind her.

"What the hell did you think you were doing?" she spits through clenched teeth.

I shake my head, hoping this is a horrible dream. "I don't know what you mean."

She grabs my ear and pulls me close. My face contorts in pain and I rise up on my toes to try and loosen her grip. Her breath is warm and smells terrible. "Don't lie to me, you little... Why did you take some of your sister's presents and put them on your side? Why?"

Her words are punchy and sharp, edged with venom as she whispers them. Confusion burns in my mind. "How did you..."

"How did I know?" she sneers. "I knew because I put them there last night, you idiot!"

"What do you mean? Did Santa..."

"Santa? Santa?" She laughs once, mocking me. "Santa doesn't exist. He isn't real. It's your worthless father and I who buy the presents and put them out for you." Her eyes are dull, absorbing the light from the kitchen window. "It's about time you knew that anyway."

She shoves me away and stands tall. I rub my ear, cowering from her. Countless thoughts tumble around in my mind. She points a threatening finger at me and says "And if you ever tell your sister what I've just told you, I'll make sure you're sorry for the rest of your life. Do I make myself clear?"

I can't look at her as I nod. I feel her eyes piercing me.

"So tell me why you did it? Was what you got not what you asked for? Did you not get everything you wanted and more? You know what?" She looks at me with complete disgust, and waves her hands in front of her. "I don't care; I actually don't care. You've proved yourself to be an ungrateful little swine. You'll be getting nothing in the future – nothing. Don't think this will be forgotten."

Santa doesn't exist. He isn't real. Her words repeat themselves over and over again. I want to scream at her how much I hate her, but I can't; the words stick in my throat.

Besides, Louise is in the living room with my dad, and I'm not going to spoil her day. Tears spring to my eyes; I don't try to stop them. Normally, when she shouts at me I try not to let her see how much she has upset me, but this time, I can't help it. *Santa isn't real.* It's like a tidal wave powering over me, drowning me. I suddenly feel guilty for what I have done in taking presents from my little sister. I move forward to go back into the living room, but one look from her and I stop where I am.

"Don't you dare go in there crying. You will *not* ruin Louise's Christmas."

"I'll give her back what I swapped," I say, and I wipe my wet eyes with the cuffs of my dressing gown.

"Indeed you will not!" my mum says, and I look at her in surprise. "If you do that, she will notice you got more than her. How are you going to explain that, eh? She is four years old, for Christ's sake. Let her play with her toys. Let her enjoy her day." She opens the door a fraction and looks at her youngest daughter. Her entire face changes; her eyes fill with life, her cheeks brighten and she smiles as she sees her. For just one time, I wish she could look at me like that.

"I'm sorry, mum." I wait on her telling me it's going to be okay. I know I've done wrong; I know I've been bad. But I've just found out Santa is actually my mum and dad. I need reassurance. I want comfort. I take a step towards her, my lower lip trembling. "I'm sorry."

Without taking her eyes off Louise, she raises her finger to me, pointing, threatening, and tells me to shut up. There is a pause as her words slice into me, cutting me open. Then she turns off the light, leaving me in darkness as she steps into the living room and closes the door behind her.

8

Her eyes opened to dazzling light. Fingers pushed at her eyelids, forcing them up as she fought to close them. She was given instruction by a voice she did not know, in a tone that gave her little choice but to obey.

"Can you squeeze my hand for me?" it asked. The light disappeared; her eyes flickered shut once more. Concentrating as much as she could, she willed her fingers to tighten, but the fact was she couldn't feel the hand she was supposed to hold. "That's great," the voice said, but as the paramedic caught his colleagues' eye, he very subtly shook his head.

"The boy," she began, but she was silenced by the paramedic. His breath was warm on her face as he leaned close to her. She could smell tuna. There was a packet of mints in her pocket he could have, but it was suddenly too much effort to do anything else but sleep. She could feel fingers press on her neck and face; again, her eyelids were prised open but no light shone this time and they were allowed to close. The voices spoke again, urgent monotones against the hushed silence of the crowd. Again, she tried to speak, but the words failed to come. 'The boy' she wanted to say; he was still at the forefront of her mind, in spite of the waves of pain. She had to know he was all right. She had to know her actions were not in vain.

Then she felt the world lurch and for a moment, she was floating. The cold, wet feeling left her for a moment, before it returned. This time, she knew, she was lying on something man-made. She heard straps being tightened, felt their tension all over her body. Slowly, *with great effort, she lifted her eyes open. The air flashed blue and black, blue and black. Things seemed slower, more restrained, like everyone was moving through water. Her head was bursting with pain; her entire body screamed out in silent agony. She tried to lift her arm, but when she couldn't do that, she tried to raise her hand; next, her fingers, then her legs – but the result was always the same. She knew for certain how badly hurt she was when she couldn't even wiggle her toes. The only part of herself she could move were her eyes. Tears came as fear gripped her.*

She heard the paramedics speak with someone, their voices calm and assured, before they vanished from her view. A face appeared out of the gloom before her, young, female. She felt a warm hand take hers. For a moment, their eyes met in recognition and everything was still.

Sophie leaned forward and gently kissed her forehead. "Thank you," she said in a voice barely above a whisper. "Thank you for saving my son."

With that, the face melted back into the night, leaving a broken body, with glistening eyes and the faintest trace of a smile on its lips.

Chapter Eight

I look around me. Smiling faces are everywhere; happy couples sit close and dance closer; disco music fills the air; and the delicious aroma of barbecued chicken and beef drifts in the breeze.

I watch the most beautiful bride I've ever seen glide as one with her new husband, the hem of her pearl-white dress floating as she spins, her tiara sparkling in the bright sunshine. As the song ends, he lifts her left hand to his lips and kisses her wedding ring. "Forever," he mouths and she wraps her bare arms around his shoulders, holding him tightly. All the guests, whether on the dance floor or sat at the side or at the bar, applaud the newlyweds. It's very difficult to take my eyes off them. True love is a beautiful thing indeed.

Louise lands clumsily on the chair beside me. "That was great!" she says, beaming, and clearly drunk. "Did you see how happy they looked?" I nod. "And did you see the guy I was dancing with?" She looks over to one of the groom's two best men, who smiles and raises his glass in her direction.

"You two were all over one another at the rehearsal dinner last night," I say and take a long sip of my wine. She kisses her hand and blows it in his direction, not taking her eyes from his as she replies, "And we were all over one another this morning, too."

She smirks, and then laughs as I slap her playfully on the shoulder. I shake my head.

"So what about you, Ice-Queen?" she asks, leaning forwards. Her words are beginning to slur together; her warm breath smells of wine. "Are you going to do anything about you-know-who? I know you like him; I can tell. Or did you just bring a photo of Robert to sit and stare at?"

She apologises as soon as the words have left her lips, holding her hands in the air. A silence falls between us, a silence that is sadly familiar. She places her hand in mine. "Maybe you should just go and have a wild time, you know? Let your hair down. Throw caution to the four winds." She drains the last of her glass. "Treat this weekend as if it were your last weekend on Earth."

I sigh. Even in her state, I know she is right. For the last seven years, I have let the memory of someone rule my life. From nothing more than a misguided sense of loyalty to something precious, I've destroyed relationships as soon as they became serious; any talk of 'our' future, or any planning more than a month ahead, and I begin the familiar process of ending things. To date, the most time I have spent with any one person is four months. As such, I'm extremely reluctant to admit liking anyone – and I never, ever make the first move. I look at my sister, her bright blue eyes sparkling in the late afternoon sun. She stares at me with complete conviction, as if the words she had just said were the most important thing she would ever say to anyone. I give her hand a little squeeze.

"Okay," I say. "I'll think about it."

"You won't regret this," she says, and kisses my cheek.

"Lou! Don't do that!" I say, wiping away the lipstick. She looks at me, confused. I smile. "I don't want to think where those lips have been."

~

As the sun begins to sink from a flawless amber and lilac sky, a waiter appears at my shoulder. "This is for you," he says, and places a drink before me. "It's from the gentleman over there. I've to pass on to you his sincerest apologies, and to ask if he may join you."

I thank the waiter and look across to the man sat at a table on the other side of the dance floor. Even though I have no idea what he is apologising for, I lift the glass in a toast; he does the same. I smile in spite of myself, and he takes this as an acceptance of his request to come to my table. Outwardly I'm calm, almost nonchalant, but inside, without reason, my heart flutters like a hundred butterflies have suddenly taken wing in my chest.

We met yesterday. His name is Jack, the other best man; the one Louise did not spend the night with. He is tall and broad-shouldered, with big hands that are surprisingly well taken care of. He is handsome. He is charming, clever and funny. He is everything I want in a man. And it's for that exact reason he is everything I cannot have.

He sits at my side. For a long moment, nothing happens; a strange silence settles between us. We watch couples dance. We watch the sun set. Then he touches his glass to mine, and with one word, changes the course of my night. He simply says, "Friends?"

At last night's rehearsal dinner, we were seated directly opposite each other. I caught him staring at me several times, never holding my eye for more than a blink, the way a schoolboy does to a girl he has a crush on. Although we didn't say a word to each other the whole evening, it wasn't long before I found myself staring back.

I nod, and look into his soft, brown eyes. "Friends, as long as you tell me why you are apologising."

His smile is warm enough to melt butter. "I wasn't being rude last night, I hope you know. I just found it difficult to look at anyone or anything else." I motion to speak, but he asks me to wait until he has finished. "When you sat down opposite me, I couldn't believe my luck. It's not every day I get to have dinner with someone as beautiful as you." I feel my cheeks redden. "I couldn't take my eyes off you. I wanted to say something, to start a conversation, but every time I tried, someone would ask me a question or would ask you what you thought of 'this' or 'that'. And before I know it, the meal is over and I'm in a taxi heading back to the hotel."

"So you're apologising for thinking I'm pretty?" I ask.

He shakes his head. "It's not that."

"Then you must be apologising for leering at me the entire evening."

His eyes widen and his jaw drops slightly. "Leering?" he whispers. He looks around to make sure no one was listening. "Do you think I was leering at you? God, no! I was maybe staring a little bit – in fact, I wouldn't even call it staring, more like 'admiring' – but that was only because I thought you were... Wait a minute," he stops as he sees the look on my face. "Are you playing with me?" I burst out laughing, and he throws his hands up in the air. "Well, that's just great!" he says. "Here I am, baring my soul to you, and all you can do is make fun of me." He folds his arms across his chest, and I place my hand on his.

"I'm sorry," I say through my laughter. "I'm really sorry."

We sit like that for a long moment, him pretending to be in a mood and me trying to stop laughing. The music flows in the warm evening air. The bride and groom wander amongst the guests. Louise has disappeared and I hesitate to think what she is up to. It's then I realise I have left my hand on his. I absently stroke his skin with my thumb.

"Okay. That was great," I say. "Thank you. I haven't laughed like that in ages!"

He smiles once more and puts his free hand over mine.

"Now, are you going to tell me what brought you here?" I

say. He looks at me, confused. "The apology; are you going to tell me why it's necessary?"

He pauses, eyebrows raised, appearing to give my question some serious thought. He sighs. I know he is simply letting the tension build. "I'm not sure how to tell you this," he starts, and then he smiles as he adds, "But I think my brother might have made a move on your little sister."

Later that night, I am on the dance floor, my head resting on his shoulder, his strong arms wrapped round my back. We don't speak; I feel his breath in my ear. My stomach lurches with every step we take. Louise's words echo in my thoughts. In two days time, I shall be on a plane, returning to a life of monotony. Maybe, I think, I should allow myself this one little luxury. He tightens his arms, pulling me closer. It is as if I am floating. *Two days*, I whisper in silence over and over again. I close my eyes and let the moment consume me.

And when I open them, we are the only ones on the dance floor. The music has stopped and everyone is watching us.

~

Once the wedding reception is over and we have waved the very happy couple off to the airport to begin their honeymoon, Jack and I return to our respective rooms and pack enough for two days and three nights. Within the hour, we are checking into a beautiful wooden lodge at the foot of the mountains. And twenty minutes later, we are asleep in each other's arms, fully-clothed, exhausted and smiling.

For forty-eight hours we are like one being, but there is no pretence about what this is for either of us. We both know that when I board the flight home, we will never see one another again. We promise not to stay in contact; these two days will be ours forever and our lives in the real world should not diminish that.

The first day, the first morning, I open my eyes to the wonderful sight of him looking at me. He is watching me sleep. *He is actually watching me sleep.* I reach across and rest my hand on his cheek. Today, there is no empty pillow, no unlived dream.

"Good morning, beautiful," he says. I smile. He leans forward and kisses me on the mouth. It's a long, tender meeting of our lips and it feels like a warm snake is climbing the length of my spine. I close my eyes, capturing this moment for all time. I know that this kiss will be the first of many, many kisses today.

We hardly leave the room on the first of our two days together. My sister's words linger in my thoughts; I release my inhibitions, let my guard down. And before the sun has set, before the day has ended, I feel something I haven't felt in a long, long time.

After a few hours sleep, we waken late and shower together, barely able to be apart for any length of time at all. By noon we stand at the base of a path that winds its way up into the mountains. The lady who works in the grocery store recommended it, telling us the view was well worth the effort. It should take us around six hours to walk, but there are plenty of places to rest and eat, and at the top there is a cable car to take us back down.

We wander up the mountain, holding hands the entire way. Jack carries the rucksack filled with provisions. I find myself unable to take my eyes off him when he speaks. And when he listens, I know he is truly listening to me, and not simply waiting for his turn to say something. We talk about everything. It is very liberating being able to share your darkest self with a virtual stranger. I tell him about Robert, of how much I loved him then and still love him now; of how I have never in my life said goodbye to anyone; of how I can never have children. I listen intently as he speaks of Lynn, his first love, his truest love, the one girl to whom no other has ever come close. Every time he mentions her name, he smiles and his eyes light up. He says he thinks about her every day, and he has done so since the day they broke up. He laughs when he says he knows he will continue to do so until the day he dies. I slide my arm around his waist, lean my head into his chest; his breaths match mine. I know exactly how he feels.

We share our entire lives that afternoon. Without thought, I offer my soul to him and he takes it, giving me his in return. We laugh at stories of our pasts, we reveal dreams of our perfect futures and we confess our deepest truths and secrets without fear of judgement. We eat under a huge tree that lets the sun's rays through in ribbons of pure gold. We drink ice-cold water from a waterfall, soaking our feet in the stream into which it drops. We make love in a clearing away from the path, silently, intensely, with the weight of nature watching. I feel myself unable to imagine a life after tonight. I hold on to every single moment, squeezing it dry, treasuring every breath.

About an hour before sunset, we reach the top. The path opens out into a shelf of rock, which overhangs the steep face below. Three benches sit perfectly spaced out behind the waist-high fence that rings the platform, and to our right, a chunk has been carved out the mountain for the cable-car to nestle into. We are alone, and we sit together on the middle bench. And we stare into heaven.

The lady in the grocery store was right – the view is nothing short of spectacular. Trees of every colour of green grow from a patchwork quilt of rolling hills that stretch to the distant horizon; a few tracers of purple cloud creep across a sky so perfect and so blue that it looks like coloured glass. Spots of rust and pink and gold are splashed across the forests as though a child has coated her paintbrush and flicked it onto the canvas before us. And the air is so fresh and clean it feels like ice when it enters my lungs.

For almost an hour we sit in silence, holding each other, the need for words gone. We watch the sun crawl across the sky, watching it change colour. And when it hits the dark edges of the forest, it explodes, filling the sky in a sudden wash of burnt red, orange, peach and amber. The forest below is a silhouette, the setting sun having drained it of life as it slid from view. This is nature at its effortless finest. The thought strikes me that this has been happening for millions of years. And tonight, I have never seen anything so humbling.

"It's just too beautiful," he says. I can tell from his voice he has a tear in his eye. The world is a blur to me, too.

I look up, to where the waves of colour melt into the darkening sky.

"A thousand blue," I whisper, my voice cracking with emotion.

"I love you too," he says, and holds me tighter. I close my eyes, and listen to the pounding in my ears. It has been a very long time since anyone has said those words to me. He has misheard me, but I don't bother correcting him, because deep down, the frozen heart of the Ice Queen has thawed, and I've fallen for him.

We take the last cable car down to the village and return to our room. It's after eleven o'clock. In nine hours I'll be on an aeroplane, alone, returning to my life of routine. I throw my arms around him, close my eyes and wish I never had to let him go.

"I don't know if I can do this," I say and suddenly, I'm sobbing uncontrollably. "I can't believe what's happened here."

He sniffs. I feel him nod. Neither of us moves for a long time. Only twice before have I ever felt so utterly helpless and stripped bare. I don't think I have ever cried so hard.

He picks me up and kisses me on the mouth as he carries me to the bed. We undress in silence. Moonlight coats the room in pale silver. And then we simply lie together, legs entwined, holding each other like letting go would be the end of us.

I want to say thank you. I want him to know how much these two days have meant to me. I want to tell him I love him. I feel sleep approach.

And I want to say what I've never said to anyone before: I want to tell him goodbye.

~

I open my eyes to a deafening, unfamiliar buzzing sound. Remembering where I am I reach over to the bedside cabinet and turn the alarm clock off. My flight leaves in two hours. Darkness fills the room. I roll over to watch my love sleeping, just as he did to me two mornings ago. My hand feels for his cheek, but finds only the cool, soft pillow. I listen to the heavy silence.

I am alone.

I turn on the light. He has gone; left while I was sleeping. Emptiness fills my heart. A jarring certainty stabs at me; I know I'll never see him again.

As I sit up, swinging my legs onto the floor, I see a folded piece of paper under the alarm clock. I hold it delicately between my fingers and take several deep breaths before I open it.

Tears splash onto the paper and I wipe them away. I lift the note to my nose and take in the last of him. I let out a long, low moan. The pain in my chest is crushing. For the last seven years I have built a wall around myself to avoid this very feeling; I chose the path of loneliness. I became the Ice-Queen.

I place the note into my purse and collapse onto the bed in floods of tears, his eight words floating in my mind.

"This way, you don't need to say goodbye."

9

The paramedics continued speaking to her as the ambulance sped to the hospital. Her sense of hearing was sharper than she could ever remember it. Every sound was amplified and became crystal clear in her mind as she drifted between light and dark, but she could not focus on any one sound above another; everything the paramedic said to her lost its importance amongst the radio chatter, the drone of the engine, the wailing siren and the regular beeping sound that echoed her heartbeat.

The bright lights and warmth of the ambulance's interior was in stark contrast to the dark, cold road she had slid to a crunching halt on. Pins and needles danced the length of her arms and hands. She could just about move her fingers – at least it felt like she could – but her legs were still as heavy as lead. Fluid seeped into her through an intravenous tube; it was like droplets of peace seeping through her veins, lending her to a sense of calm and resignation. She closed her eyes once more. Everything smelled and tasted like blood.

"Can you squeeze my hand for me? That's great, thanks. A little bit tighter. Excellent! You're doing really well. Can you look at me now? I need you to look at me. Open your eyes. Open. Open. That's it. Do you know what's happened? Do you remember where you are? You were in an accident. You were hit by a car and you're in an ambulance. My name is Emily and we're taking you to hospital. The noises you can hear are – no, *no, try to keep your eyes open, that's a girl – the noises you can hear are the siren and the monitor we've attached you to. I don't want you to worry. We'll be there in a few minutes and get you... Keep your eyes open. Keep them open. What's your name? Tell me what..."*

Chapter Nine

I am on holiday with my friends, abroad for the first time and without any of my family for the first time, too.

For the better part of two weeks, the five of us have drunk wine, sunbathed by the pool during the day, and at night let our inhibitions loose on the dance floors of the local pubs and clubs. I've spent a fortune, but I haven't stopped smiling once. A whole year of saving and sacrifice has been well worth it.

It's the day before we leave, and we are on an outing with the travel company reps to an island a few miles off the coast. It's paradise. Palm trees sprout at impossible angles from sand as white as snow, strange and beautiful butterflies land on flowers of every colour imaginable, and further in, crystal clear water tumbles down slate-grey rocks into a lagoon as green as the purest emerald. On the beach, the organisers are preparing a lunch-time barbecue. It won't be ready for half an hour or so, and my friends and I take the opportunity to indulge in a spot of snorkelling in the shallows just off the coastline.

Only three of us don the masks and breathing tubes; the other two decide their time would be better spent topping up their already glorious tans. We wade into the sea, and despite the scorching heat in the air, the water bites our ankles with sharp teeth. "It's freezing," I shout, which is a huge mistake. No sooner had the words left my mouth, than one of the crew from the boat (a gorgeous man, bronzed and muscular, with piercing blue eyes and a heart-melting smile) sprints towards me, picks me up in his arms and marches out until the water is up to his waist. In spite of my squeals of terror, I can hear everyone laugh from the beach. "Save me!" I yell, "Please someone save me!" and echoes of the past, of my sister and my uncle sound in my mind. But my knight in shining armour doesn't come, and I am unceremoniously thrown into the cold, cold sea.

I surface quickly, my feet finding the soft, sandy floor. All eyes are on me, and a few of the other guests on the trip are clapping. I wave to them, smiling. "You should come in! The water is lovely!" And with that, I place the mouthpiece between my teeth, slide the mask over my eyes and nose, turn and dive into the blue.

The current is surprisingly strong, and my friends and I allow ourselves to drift along with it, studying the wonder of the seabed six feet below, before swimming back to where we started. Tiny fish dart between us, glowing in the filtered sunlight. Plants sway as if caught in an underwater breeze. Stones and shells litter the sand in a truly beautiful collection of colours. An idea strikes me: I always buy my little sister a present if I go away on trip. I have already bought her a t-shirt, but that's becoming boring – I always get her a t-shirt. Wouldn't it be lovely if I brought her back something different, something utterly unique? I smile at the thought, and begin searching the sand.

Before long, I find what I'm looking for. A rock the size of my fist hides between long stems of purple seaweed, and I turn to face into the flow, not taking my eyes off the rock for a second in case I lose it. With a deep breath through the snorkel, I dive. Without any weights to help me sink, I kick my feet and propel myself downwards with my hands sweeping the sea behind me. It seems to take forever and my arms burn as I fight against the current. My fingers grab the ends of the seaweed and I pull myself further down. The rock – my rock – is less than a foot away now, and I can't believe how stunning it is. Red and gold circles, outlined in white, dot a pale green base that looks as smooth as glass. There is nothing I have seen to compare to it. I think of Louise, of her face as she holds it. I will tell her how I had to swim down further than the truth to get it. I will make a story of it, and I know she will appreciate it. I reach forward and touch it.

With a sudden, terrifying quickness, it moves, darting up and away from me with a speed that defies belief. I gasp in fright, turning away from it, the last of the air in my lungs leaving my body in bubbles through the tube in my mouth. A cloud of black surrounds me, blocking out the light and I kick my feet to escape it. My shoulder hits the sand. My lungs ache. I have no idea where the surface is. The ink drifts through my fingers. It's gritty. I need to breathe. I'm being spun around by the current. Where is the light? I feel around for the floor, but my arms flail aimlessly. I really need to breathe. I didn't realise how cold it's become. I feel faint. I close my eyes.

~

From clear water, I watch my body, myself, struggle against the wash of darkness that envelopes it. I see its fingers rake at the sea, grasping for something that isn't there. It thinks it is drowning. I can feel its pain, but it doesn't hurt me; I can sense its fear, but it doesn't scare me. One single thought runs through my mind: *You can't die yet. You can't let go until you tell him goodbye* and it repeats itself over and over again. I wait for the stillness, for the fighting to stop, and then I move.

Calmly, effortlessly, I swim towards myself. The octopus pulses by my head in a flash of colour, but it won't know I'm here. I watch it pass, more afraid than the body before me. I take my time. *You can't let go until you tell him goodbye.* My arms wrap around cold shoulders and I lift upwards. As my skin breaks the surface, as sunlight drowns me, I let myself become one once more with my body.

~

Gasping, I open my eyes to the light of a thousand shimmering suns. A soft breeze blows across my face, cooling against the intense afternoon heat. A perfect, cloudless sky arcs over me, infinite and ethereal, and I reach my hand out to touch it, my silhouetted fingers clawing at empty air. It takes me a second or two to realise where I am, to remember what happened. My snorkel is gone, lost to the sea, but the mask remains around my eyes. I look around, treading water. The island is a short distance away, but the beach where everyone is has disappeared. The current, it seems, has carried me further round the island and away from them.

I kick for the shore. My entire body burns as the oxygen returns to my blood, but within a few short minutes I'm lying on the sand, filling my lungs in greedy gulps of fresh air until my breathing returns to normal. I tear the mask from my face and let it fall. My mouth tastes of salt. My eyes are slits against the pure blue brightness above me. But the smile I wear is even more luminous than the sun. I'm alive!

The knowledge that I nearly died sits at the front of my thoughts. In fact, I know I should be dead – the last thing I consciously remember was not being able to find the surface – but there is something else, a dream that feathers my imagination. Or is it a memory? I can see myself almost drown, then somehow my arms lift the limp body up through the dark cloud. I spoke; the voice in my head was my own; I remember the words I used, which is the strangest thing of all.

I shake the confusion from my mind and sit upright. I

yawn, tilting my head to one side, then the other, letting the water dribble out of my ears.

A memory surfaces from a long time ago, a memory of my uncle telling me how he once fell from a wall and landed on his head. Although he was unconscious, he said he remembered holding his own hand, telling himself not to worry, that he wasn't going to die. I loved my uncle with every fibre of my being, and even though I never questioned anything he told me, I always doubted the sincerity of that particular story. Now, I find myself wishing I had asked him more about it.

I stand up, brushing the sand from the backs of my shoulders and legs. The pain has gone; my lungs no longer feel as though they are on fire. I look to the horizon. A thousand blue stares back at me, and I smile. I think, maybe, something amazing has just happened to me.

A bird cries from the jungle-like growth behind me, snapping me back to reality. The others will be looking for me now, and I start walking in the direction of their beach. I have taken no more than a few steps when I remember my face-mask. As I bend down to pick it up, I freeze. Lying beside it, completely exposed, alien against the yellow sand, is a pale green rock as smooth as glass, with red and gold circles outlined in white.

10

There was a loud crash as she was shoved through the doors of the hospital's accident and emergency department. The overwhelming brightness burned red through her eyelids and made her squeeze them shut even tighter. More voices sounded, urgent, direct, but their clipped staccato use of numbers and readings meant nothing to her. She was being wheeled very quickly to her destination, the trolley she was on jarring every time she passed through a doorway. She opened her eyes as much as she could, and through those tiny slits the ceiling lights sped by like an illuminated train, glowing yellow and white, yellow and white. Then she felt a hand on her cheek, and her eyes met those of the woman from the ambulance. Her name was Emily, she remembered. Emily. Then she remembered the wine bottle crack as it hit the pavement. She remembered the contents of the shopping bags, and thought of the dinner she would never make. And she remembered the card; her carefully chosen words explaining her news to him in a way she couldn't do face-to-face.

"You take care now", Emily said, bringing her back to reality. "The doctors and nurses will look after you from here."

She wanted to say 'thank you', but the plastic oxygen mask made her voice all but silent. Sleep. All she wanted to do was to sleep. Her eyelids grew heavy. As Emily's face slipped from view, another's replaced it.

She heard something about a cerebral contusion, felt her

eyelids be prised open and flinched as a bright light was beamed into the unprotected pupils. Then slowly, effortlessly, she let the darkness consume her once more.

Chapter Ten

I stand at the bottom of my garden, shielding my eyes against the bright morning sky. My dad tells me to move right, then left, to stand up straighter; my mum comes over and pulls my blazer down or flicks her fingers through my red hair or straightens my tie. Ben is in his kennel, barking every few seconds to remind us he is tied up. Louise runs around trying to catch a butterfly. I notice my dad pays more attention to her than to me, but it doesn't really bother me; I just wish he would look in my direction from time to time, too.

"Are you ready?"

I nod.

"Big smiles, then! Say 'cheese'!"

The camera clicks once, then twice, and continues to do so until the film is spent. There are only a few photos of me on my own; the rest of them have my sister, or Ben, or both of them in with me. I know already that the picture they'll choose to frame and sit above the fireplace will not be one of me on my own.

My dad gives me a kiss on the cheek and wishes me good luck, then takes Louise and Ben into the house. I slide my arms into the straps of my bag, take my mum's hand and together, we walk down the road to begin my first day of school.

At the gates, the teachers are there to welcome us and show us where to go. I see a few of my friends from nursery, and we wave at each other with one hand, the other clamped around our mum's. They are dressed like I am: shiny black shoes, white knee-length socks and shirt, dark-grey skirt and blazer, and a tie striped in the school colours of blue and green. We form a line at the big main doors to the building. The grown-ups are smiling and laughing, but my friends all seem scared, their eyes wide as though tears are only seconds away. I wonder if I look as they do.

Once inside, we are led into the classroom. I sit at one of the circular tables, still wearing my bag around my shoulders, still wearing my blazer. I can't read yet, but I know what my name looks like and it is written on a sheet of card in front of me. Two of my friends sit next to me. Three boys sit across from us; I only know one of them. The parents are stood at the back of the room. One of my friends grins at her mum and dad, and they wink at her. I try to catch my mum's eye, but she is staring out the window at something. The teacher claps her hands and the buzz in the room dies to silence.

"My name," she says in a sweet, kind voice, "is Miss David. Every morning, when we come inside and sit down, I will say 'good morning, children', and you will say 'good morning, Miss David'. Shall we practice? And shall we ask the mums and dads to join in?"

When she speaks the daily greeting, her tone lifts and lowers as if she were singing. On the first try, it's only the adults who reply, some of the children managing to mumble, but nothing more. After a few attempts, and without the help of the adults, we are wishing our new teacher a good morning as though we have been doing it all our lives.

Soon, it is time for the parents to leave, and they file out the room in one steady stream. Some give little waves to their children, some blow kisses. My mum keeps her eyes fixed straight ahead of her, not once acknowledging me as she passes by within touching distance. Maybe, I think, she didn't see me.

At first, only a couple of sniffs are heard as the door closes behind them and Miss David stands alone in front of the huge blackboard. But then, as realisation dawns that they are not coming back in, the children begin to cry.

I look around me. Almost everyone is in tears, some making more of a display of their feelings than others. I feel my bottom lip curl and my eyes sting, but I'm not sad because I miss my mum or because I want her to come back.

I'm crying because I don't.

~

Darkness grows, the audience falls silent and two thousand eyes stare straight ahead. An orchestra sounds from within two huge speakers; three beams of bluish light land as one, circular on the stage, illuminating a solitary figure. The music builds to a crescendo, and then fades to almost nothing. Louise looks up, opens her arms and sings.

My mum and dad sit either side of me and we are only three rows from the front. My sister's voice carries over my head, filling the hall with effortless ease. Around me, I hear gasps from strangers, whispers of disbelief and wonder at the beauty of what they hear – but I am not shocked; I am used to how it sounds. She is only thirteen, yet she performs like she has been doing so forever.

The song she sings tells of a love lost, and although she has absolutely no experience of this in itself, her words are so compelling, the story so emotive, that people beside me wipe quickly at damp cheeks. For me, I simply cannot take my eyes off her.

Her white linen dress ripples at the hem as she sways in time with the music. At home, practising, she realised she did not need exaggerated hand gestures or, indeed, to even move her feet during the song; the lyrics, the melody and more importantly, her voice, would be more than enough for those watching.

As the song nears its end, I feel myself mouthing the words, and to my surprise, my mum gives me a little nudge, looks at me and smiles. "Amazing," she says, and I nod, smiling back.

Finally, as her last note fades to nothing, as the spotlight dies and darkness consumes every corner of the hall, the audience erupts in a wave of deafening applause. When the lights burn once more, there are those who are so moved by what they have heard that they are standing. I am one of them. She takes her acclaim and almost skips off the stage in joy.

Louise is the last to sing and there is a short interval as the judges decide who is to be the winner. In my mind, there is only one.

I am not wrong.

She accepts her award and stands at the microphone, waving to the crowd before her, waiting for the applause to settle before she speaks.

"Thank you," she says once the hall falls silent. "I really don't think I deserve this," and looks at the trophy in her hands. "But I would like to say something, if I may. A year ago, the thought of me singing in front of anyone was too frightening to contemplate; I had very little self-confidence and even less belief that I had could actually sing – in fact, that hasn't changed much!" The audience laughs obediently. "But one person made me realise that, at the very least, I might make a few people happy. She listened to me, gave me her thoughts without ever hurting me, and she helped me overcome my fears. But far more importantly, in the process, she became my best friend." With one hand, she holds the golden, twin-handed cup above her head. "This is for my sister. Thank you."

She takes a step back from the microphone as applause and cheering fills the hall. I feel my parents' eyes burn through me. Pride emanates from me in waves; a sense of belonging fills me in a way I could not imagine. Surprisingly, I don't cry – I want to, but I can't. My mum puts her arm around my shoulders and holds me close. My dad leans over and kisses my cheek. They are both, it seems, as proud of me as they are of Louise.

It has taken almost sixteen years, but tonight, at a school talent contest, for the very first time in my life, I have acceptance.

~

I lie on my back, alone, cushioned by a deep carpet of scented grass. A sympathetic breeze feathers my skin, carrying the silence of the horizon. Warm air enters me, leaves me, in equal measure. Everything is still. Something unseen brushes the palm of my hand. Slowly, my eyelids open.

All the blues there have ever been, or ever will be, hover high above me in a seamless wash. I stare into infinity, losing myself. My aunt's words trickle through my thoughts, and I smile without moving my lips: There are so many more than a thousand. A light dusting of silver speckles the sky like tiny holes in the curtain of night, and the more I look, the more the heavier shades chase those lighter to the void, the more of them I see.

My breathing remains calm and even. My bones are leaden, sinking into the earth. Peace wraps itself around me, coiling my body in an endless ribbon of silk. I sense my heart beating, for I cannot feel it or hear it.

And then, only then, I allow myself to remember him, his memory returning to me in molten waves through my veins. I close my eyes against the pain and let the liquid fire consume me, melting the wall of ice that stands guard over my soul. His scent replaces the air around me. His fingers trace the path of forever on my bare skin. His breath is warm on the curve of my neck. His voice echoes, a whisper, a roar, telling me he'll love me for all time. I reach out to him for one last touch, one final feel of his skin before…

Silent tears spill, landing softly on the grass. I sob until there is nothing left, until my face stings as the cooling night bites it. The sky feels closer to me than he is now.

And in the quiet of a late summers' evening, as my defences are built back up stronger than before, I repeat my vow to never love again.

11

She was asleep as she watched herself from the other side of the operating theatre.

A nurse stood over her, patiently observing the machine that fed air to her lungs via a tube down her throat. A heart-rate monitor sounded, electronically mimicking the dull thud with monotonous, hypnotic beeps. Men and women in green scrubs crowded round her. They spoke in quiet, determined voices, their every word crucial; they moved in beautiful harmony, a ballet-like performance of grace and purpose that exuded knowledge and confidence. They, she knew, were trying to save her.

Her blood-stained clothes were covered by fresh green sheet. Her eyelids were taped shut, her skin the colour of ash, and were it not for the flurry of activity surrounding her she would easily have passed as dead. The surgeons worked on her shaved skull, but she didn't care about the hair loss. She had to make it through the surgery alive. She had to see him at least one more time. There was so much she wanted to say, so many things he had to know and her thoughts chased each other through her subconscious mind like fireflies at dusk.

She watched the surgeons weave their magic, she watched the monitors as they flashed her condition to the assembled group and she watched the girl on the table, lying still and all but lifeless and knew she had to do something.

"We need to stem the bleed," a voice spoke from behind a mask.

"Blood pressure at one-twenty over eighty and falling," said another.

"Pass me the clamp." It was the first voice again.

"She's slipping; systolic at ninety-five; ninety; eighty… We're losing her."

The constant beeping of the heart-rate monitor slowed to a halt, before sounding a continuous drone that sent the medical group into yet another finely practised drill. As they moved as one, as they prepared to shock her heart into starting again, she watched them and knew immediately what she must do.

Chapter Eleven

In the four short months since the Christmas dance, Robert and I have become inseparable. We are very much in love. He is my constant companion and my dearest friend. I need him with every fibre of my body, and care for him more deeply than I ever thought possible. My heart aches when we are apart and I feel my soul reaching for him when we are together. My friends wish they could have what we have. Every kiss still feels like the first. Soon, I know, it will be time for us to take things further.

Tomorrow is his mum's birthday, and we are out shopping for a gift. He has left it until the last minute, and I spend most of the morning asking him how he can be so ill-prepared. "It's the same day every year," I say, to which he says nothing, but shrugs his shoulders and kisses me instead. Her husband has bought them tickets for a show, so they will be away for the night, which means we have to get something for her this morning and give her it before she leaves. He wants to get her a piece of jewellery, and we scour the mall, looking for a present that he says can be from both of us; something unique, something different – something she will want to keep forever. He asks me to choose it, trusting my judgement as a female. I remind him I'm not really in touch with forty year-old women's fashion, and although I think his mum is wonderful, I don't feel confident in selecting something that would match her tastes, but he insists nonetheless.

We stroll through the stores, arm-in-arm, hardly paying attention to what we should be looking at, more intent on simply being together. I breathe him in, falling for him more and more. People smile at us as we walk past them. We smile back and say hello. It seems to brighten their moment, and it makes us happy, too. When other couples see us, they reach for one another's hands, or suddenly feel the need to kiss their partner's cheek. Our love, it appears, is infectious.

We spend the morning searching the jewellery stores, but finding nothing. As lunch-time approaches, we visit the only one left. It's tiny compared to the more established names, and the displays are tired-looking and dated, but there is something very welcoming about the place. From behind a glass counter, at the back of the shop, the lone salesman asks us if he can help. He is an elderly man. Wisps of white hair above his ears dance, blown by a fan at his side; his otherwise bald head shines pink in the soft light. He smiles at us as we approach. His eyes are like chips of blue ice, alive and intense, yet disarming and trustworthy. I like him and immediately smile back. I try to explain what we are searching for, even though we don't really know in any detail, and as I'm speaking, he looks at Robert. Something passes between them then, something unspoken, there one instant, gone the next. He steps back and clasps his hands in front of him. The grin he wears reaches from ear to ear.

"I see," he says, staring kindly at me. "If you will be good enough to wait here for a moment, I'll be right back." He looks at us each in turn, still grinning and sighs happily before disappearing through a door behind him.

"He's nice," I say to Robert. He holds me tighter and kisses my forehead. I lean into him. I love this boy, this man, so very, very much.

When the jeweller returns, he carries a red velvet box, four inches square. He holds it carefully, his old fingers barely touching the edges. He looks to me, then to Robert, then back to me. "This is the one for you," he says, and lifts the lid.

Inside, a necklace hangs from two tiny hooks. A single teardrop-shaped diamond is suspended from a polished silver chain, gleaming against the deep-red base. As he slowly turns the case, the light catches the stone, and it twinkles blue and gold and white as though coated in stardust. I feel my eyes grow large and my mouth open.

"It's beautiful," I say, looking at once to Robert, then quickly add, "no, it's beyond even that."

The old man smiles anew. "I'm sure she'll love it," he whispers, and gently closes the box. I'm not even sure Robert saw the necklace – his eyes were on me the entire time I was looking at the piece – but he takes out his wallet and replies, "Yes, sir, I'm sure she will."

~

We wave his parents off, watching from the doorway as the car reverses up the sloped driveway and disappears down the road. He turns to me and smiles, then grabs me in a huge hug and kisses me on the mouth. "You're all mine now," he says, and I kiss him back. My eyes are closed and I taste the promise on his lips. "Will you stay the night?"

I want to nod, to agree, to let him know that tonight will be ours forever, but I can't. I won't put myself under that pressure. "We'll see," I say, and he groans playfully.

"We'll see," he repeats, and we walk into the house together, leaving the night behind us.

In the living room, I kick my shoes off and throw myself backwards onto the leather couch. Robert picks up the telephone and walks to the dining room. "Chinese?" he asks, and begins to dial. I don't need to reply – he knows it's my favourite takeaway, and he knows what I always have. He places the order, but as he hangs up the phone, he moans in dismay. "Oh, come on!" he says, coming back into the living room. I sit up. He is carrying a pale pink holdall. It's his mums. He sits beside me and opens it. There are a few items of clothing and things like deodorant, hairspray, and a little bag of make-up.

"They'll come back for it, won't they?" I ask, not fully understanding why he is so upset.

"Yes, I'm sure they will." He shakes his head in disappointment. "That's the point."

"Robert," I say, and put my hand on his knee, "I'm afraid you've lost me."

He puts the bag on the carpet and slides in close. His eyes are sad. "Think about it. This is the first time you and I have been alone together; the first time my parents have gone away overnight since we've become a couple. They know how I feel about you, and they also know that I've never... You know..." His hands flap at invisible circles.

The smile I wear seems only to add to his discomfort. "I know."

"So, it's pretty obvious that they've left this bag here deliberately so they need to come home after the show. That way, we can't..."

"They might come back before it," I interrupt, and he sighs. I squeeze his thigh. "Anyway, we can't do anything about it, can we? Let's just enjoy our dinner and the pleasure of each others' company."

He turns to me and apologises. In a heartbeat, his mood changes; his gorgeous smile returns, his eyes light up and as he looks at me, I feel as though I am the only person in the world.

~

We lie on the couch together, the taste of our meal fading to memory with every moment. The television is on, soundless and bright, but neither of us pays it any attention. For a long while we lie on our sides, our thoughts and dreams exchanged through warm whispered breaths and soft kisses. As time passes, as the talking ceases, he carefully lies on top of me. I wrap my legs around his; I feel him through his jeans, feel him press into me. His lips linger on mine, moist and warm, and each flick of his tongue sends cold shivers through my bones. I hold him close. He runs delicate fingertips across my cheek and into my hair, kissing my neck, gently biting my ear. My skin feels tight. He tells me he loves me, over and over again. My voice is an echo of his. Our breaths are heavy, as one. My heart feels like it will implode at any instant. My hands are under his shirt; his skin is smooth and I trace the length of his spine. He is shaking. I close my eyes tighter. The world is in darkness, yet I see everything with star-bright clarity. I'm floating. There is an ache inside I have never known before. A single truth cascades over me, drowning me in the certainty of what tonight will bring. My heels touch. He presses into me once more. My body burns as if a thousand hot needles have pierced me at once. I open my eyes.

"Robert," I manage, though I'm breathing hard. He looks at me with so much care in his eyes I could melt into the leather creases of the couch.

"Are you all right?" he asks, his voice filled with concern.

I smile and kiss him hard on the mouth. "Of course I am, silly. I just need to use the bathroom."

Upstairs, I quickly visit his bedroom, and then go to the bathroom. I lock the door and strip naked, placing my clothes in a neat pile on the floor. A river of ice has replaced the blood in my veins, and I struggle to keep my hands steady. I put the white dressing gown I took from his bedroom over my shoulders and tie the belt loosely around my waist. I take deep breath after deep breath. This will happen just once in my life, I tell myself. There is only one first time.

At the top of the stairs, I say his name and he comes out from the living room and looks up at me. "There's a spider in the bathroom," I say. I don't think he's noticed I'm wearing his dressing gown. "Would you get it for me?"

He leaps up the stairs two at a time. He definitely doesn't realise I'm not wearing my clothes. I smile in spite of myself. He is in for a shock.

I enter the bathroom behind him and close the door. I pull on the cord at my side and the room plunges into black. He mutters his confusion in short, broken words and clipped sentences. I'm still smiling. He really does have no idea. I lean forward and kiss his mouth, telling him to hush. His arms slide round my waist and I sense his surprise as he feels the soft, towelling fabric beneath his fingers. His face is lit in soft orange by a streetlight and I watch as realisation dawns on him. I undo the belt and let the gown drop to the floor. Immediately, his eyes look down the length of my bare skin. I'm trembling. Nerves, fear and excitement buffet my body. His eyes are like saucers as he hurriedly strips. I place my hands on his cheeks and tell him to slow down. He apologises, tripping over his words, and stands like a lost little boy with his arms at his sides. He makes me smile so much; I can't believe how in love with him I am.

I finish unbuttoning his shirt and undo the belt of his trousers. He kisses me softly now, tenderly, but with an expectant passion I have never known.

We stand naked, our bodies pressed together, bare skin on bare skin, and he holds me. I rest my head on his chest, feeling his pounding heart thrum through us both. His arms cling to me, his fingers trying to cover every inch of flesh. He whispers he loves me over and over again. We tremble as one.

"Are you sure?" he asks. "Are you sure you want this?"

"I'm positive," I say, knowing I have never spoken words more true. "Do you?"

We kiss and smile at each other. Of course he does.

We are about to leave the bathroom for his bedroom, when we hear a noise. It's a low, deep hum, getting louder. Then it stops and two clicks are followed by two muted bangs. Our eyes meet. The same thought passes between us: a car pulling into the driveway, its' doors opening and closing.

It's his parents. They're back.

We move like lightning. He grabs his trousers and pulls them on, telling me to lock the door and get changed. Ignoring his socks and underwear, he buttons his shirt as he darts down the stairs. In less than fifteen seconds, he is sitting on the couch, slightly out of breath and I am almost fully clothed. I pull on the cord and squint my eyes against the sudden flare of light. I sit on the edge of the bath, letting my breath return to a natural rhythm. My ears strain, listening for voices, but there is nothing. And I wait.

After a minute or so, Robert knocks on the door. He wears a look of disbelief, his lop-sided smile telling me he knows something I don't. I glance behind him, down the stairs and into the silence below.

"I don't understand," I begin. "Where are your mum and dad?"

He stifles a laugh. "Listen," he says, and he lifts his finger to his lips.

Within a few moments, I hear it again: a low, deep hum, stopping, before the two sets of soft banging sounds. I search his eyes, aware of the confusion painted on my face. He grins wildly, now.

"What room is directly below us?" he asks.

I think about it for a second or so. "The kitchen?"

He nods. "And which appliance in the kitchen has a motor, one that fires to life every few minutes?"

I shake my head. He takes me by the hand, still smiling, and leads me downstairs. In the kitchen, we wait. The clock above the door ticks round, the only break in the heavy silence. He stares at me, stifling a laugh.

Then the noise we heard when we were upstairs begins again. And my eyes immediately go to its' source: the fridge.

I look at him, disbelief in my eyes. He is laughing now. I check out the window for any sign of a car, but there is none.

"You mean…" I begin, but he kisses me before I can finish. We both laugh, and soon there are tears running down our cheeks. Not ten minutes ago, we were about to give ourselves to one another for the first time; now, we sit with our back against the kitchen units, holding hands, sharing in the funniest thing that's ever happened to me in all my sixteen years.

12

With nothing more than a thought she was at her side, ghost next to flesh and blood. She stared at the ashen face, at the grey-blue lips drained of life, at the porcelain skin that was scraped and bruised and she smiled. She understood what the outcome would be and her smile was a mix of happiness for the life she had lived and sadness for a future she would not have much of.

The doctors and nurses buzzed around her like insects. The heart-rate monitor continued its deathly monotone. Two paddles were placed on her exposed chest; on command, everyone stood back, and her body jerked violently as the electric current surged through her. Still, the sound remained. Her life slipped away.

She leaned forward then, identical faces mere inches apart. She held her hand, gently as you would a flower, and felt the warmth dissipate. The smile stayed fastened to her lips as all around her, the worried eyes of the medical team looked on. Again, the lifeless body was subjected to the shock, and again, the drone continued.

She closed her eyes, and waited. With gentle strokes, she began to will the life back into herself, her lips moving in silent prayer. "You can't die yet," she was saying. "You can't let go until you tell him goodbye." She heard a voice, male, authoritative, saying "one last time, then" and she felt herself become one with her body. The paddles pulsed, and the life-

affirming beep sounded louder and more pronounced than ever before.

With barely a pause, the surgeon was back at work, the anaesthetist continued to monitor her breathing, the nurses busied round her again, checking tubes and filling out charts. And in all their efforts to preserve her life, not one of them noticed the faintest trace of a smile play at the edges of her lips.

Chapter Twelve

Louise nudges me with her shoulder and tells me to cheer up.

"Maybe we're going on a holiday," she says excitedly. "Or we could be moving. Or what if we had a distant relative who has died and left us a fortune?"

I smile in spite of how I feel inside; her innocence is remarkable.

"Louise, I'm not sure what's going on. I mean, when have they ever asked us to be here, like this, for them both to talk to us?" She lifts her eyebrows and tilts her head. "I'm not convinced this will be a happy conversation. But at the same time, I could be wrong, and maybe we did have a secret great-aunt, whom we've never met and who's left us both millions. But the bottom line is I don't know why we're here. So let's not get our hopes up, okay?"

She shakes her head and bounces her legs excitedly. "I'm going to buy a pony."

Before I can say or do anything else, our mum and dad walk into the living room and sit on the sofa to our right. He smiles at his youngest daughter and she grins at him in return. "How's things with Robert?" he asks me. I blush, not expecting the question. I tell him everything is great, and he gives me a half-smile, staring into the fireplace. "That's good," he says."Good for you."

"I'm meeting him tonight, after this," I say, and my mum, to no one in particular, says, "Well at least you'll have something to talk about." Her eyes are hollow, sunken and dark. She has been crying – lots.

Louise clasps her hands between her springing knees and puts her mouth to my ear, whispering so only I can hear, "Pony!"

The four of us sit in expectant silence for a long moment. I feel my sister's burning enthusiasm, but I also read the body language of my parents. I know something is definitely amiss. Outside, rain lashes the window in a steady rhythm. I turn and watch dark beads hover on the glass before racing each other to the bottom, some joining together as they do so. The sky is almost black, heavy with thunderheads, low and threatening. They make me feel claustrophobic. I face my family once more. Looking from my mother to my father and back again, I realise it's not the weather which makes me feel so tense.

"Your mum and I," he begins, "have something to ask you."

"Oh, so we're asking them now, are we?" My mum's words cut the air like a scythe. Dad ignores her.

"We want to know how you would feel if…" He trails off, as if unable to finish the sentence. Louise has stopped bouncing. She too can feel the oppression in the room thicken with every heartbeat. He looks to her, and then to me, before his eyes finally settle on a spot on the floor between his feet.

"Your father has decided to leave." My mum's eyes fix on her husband as she speaks to us. They don't move as she takes a sip of tea from her mug. "He'll be gone by the morning."

Louise makes a noise, somewhere between a laugh and a gasp. "You're kidding, right?" She leans forward. "Dad, tell me she's kidding."

He shakes his head slowly.

My head feels strange, fuzzy, and spongy. I don't feel part of things at the moment, as though I'm in a dream. Louise speaks, but her words are lost to me. The last time I felt like this, the police told me my uncle was dead. A torrent of emotions cascade through me; a thousand questions leap to my throat at once. My mum and dad are splitting up. I don't know anyone else whose parents have divorced. I look at my mum. Her eyes are cold as she stares at my dad, and her face is expressionless. He, in turn, stares at the floor. Louise is still speaking, gesturing to each of them. I hear my name. It's my sister; she's asking me something. She tugs on the sleeve of my top. I turn to look at her. She is only thirteen. She dotes on my dad, and she and my mum are like best friends, too. I realise this will be almost impossible for her to comprehend.

It's my mum who speaks next, before I get a chance to ask my sister what she was saying. "Are you going to tell them why you're leaving?" Her tone is flat and emotionless, the words delivered in clipped staccato. "Or shall I?"

My dad comes over and hunkers down in front of us. His voice is low, almost apologetic. "I've met someone else," he says, and looks at us in turn.

From the corner of my eye, I catch my mum wiping her cheeks with the flat of her hand. I look at her, at the hurt and rejection on her face and I feel such pity for her I could burst. My dad is making this about himself. It's not – it's not even about Louise and I – it's about my mum. I've known for years that my dad has had affairs. His job has taken him away, sometimes for weeks at a time, and he and mum would always have a few days of hostility until she got used to the idea he was hers again. Once, he brought us back presents from a trip. As Louise was opening hers, I asked him what mine was, before the wrapper was off. I could tell by his silence that he had absolutely no idea; his girlfriend had obviously done his shopping for him. I've lost count of the number of times he has been caught out, and I used to blame my mum for sticking with him all these years; but now, seeing the pain emanate from her in waves, imagining her feelings of despair and betrayal, hopelessness and loss, I think I understand why.

"You're not really leaving, are you?" Louise's voice is as a child's. "Is it something I've done?" She holds her hands out for him to take, and he does so. His thumbs stroke her palms. He smiles, but there are tears in his eyes. I have never seen my dad cry, not at anything, not ever. Suddenly, I can't see. I hear my sister sniff. My tongue licks the saltwater from my lips. Before my dad can say anything else, I stand up and quickly leave the room, grabbing my coat from the hook on the wall, and slamming the door behind me.

I run through the pouring rain. In seconds I'm completely drenched. Fat rain splashes down hard on the pavement, making little rivers that race alongside me. I'm crying freely, now. I feel terrible for leaving my sister to deal with things on her own, but I'm not sure what I can say to make her feel any better. The fact my dad was actually crying makes me worse. But it's my mum; how can she be breathing with the amount of hurt she must feel inside right now?

I run to my Robert. The cold rain stings my cheeks, my sodden clothes stick to my skin, and my lungs burn. I run to him to feel his arms around me and to feel the touch of his lips on mine. I run to him to share with him the news that my family is no more. But most of all, with the image of my mother's face spurring me on, I run to him to hear him say he'll never, ever leave me.

~

It's been three years since my mum and dad split up, their divorce being celebrated separately but in equal measures last spring. For her part, once the initial shock subsided, she discovered a world she did not know existed. She made new friends, got promoted at work, lost loads of weight and began having fun. And even though I would stop just short of saying we are friends, our relationship has definitely improved. For his, nothing in his life changed except the people. It was like redecorating a room – the layout of things remains identical (his new partner, Angela, has two girls, younger than Louise and I by four or five years each) but the walls are different and there's freshness in the air. Very quickly, he slipped into his role of provider and absentee-father; he was reliving the past, but ignored the lessons learnt.

They were married during the summer, in a quiet ceremony held in a registry office. Louise was there, but only as a regular guest – our two new stepsisters were the only bridesmaids. I couldn't make it. I was on my first holiday abroad without my family, almost drowning in the sea. To this day, I'm convinced Angela hid a smile when I told her I wouldn't be attending.

My dad phoned me last night and asked me to meet him. We haven't spoken much since before the wedding, and I stare out into the cold from the coffee shop window, wondering what could be so important. He's late, but he always is, and his coffee sits steaming in front of me. It will be cold by the time he drinks it.

He arrives a few minutes after I have drained the last of my Latte and ordered another, looking pensive as he strolls through the carpet of rust and copper leaves that separate the car park from the building. Even from here, his eyes are dark and distant, and troubled lines furrow his brow. My heart sinks. The last time I seen him look like this – indeed, the only time – was when he told us he was leaving home, and I quickly suppress the memories of that day.

My dad takes his seat opposite me and sips his coffee. "Cold," he says. "I should've been on time, I suppose." The smile he flashes would disarm the staunchest defence, and he winks at me.

For a few minutes, we chat about our lives: My job; his job; my sister; his sore back. But when I can wait no longer, I ask him why he's really here.

He stares vacantly at a spot on the wall over my shoulder. For a few seconds, as he plays out the conversation in his mind, subtle changes mark his face. He takes too long in choosing the words. This, I know, will not be a happy talk and I feel the wall of ice that surrounds my emotions strengthen.

"Angela and I", he begins, "have been talking. Recently, she's been struggling with my past, and she doesn't know how to deal with it."

"Your past? What does she mean?"

A rueful smile crosses his lips, a flicker of regret. "I made a decision when she and I first met. I told her everything, and I mean everything. All the things I had ever done, good and bad..."

"Mostly bad!"

"Mostly bad... fair enough." He smiles with his eyes at my understanding of things. "But now she is scared I will revert to my 'bad old ways'. At the beginning it wasn't so much of an issue – we were too busy trying to be together and to work out our future to let the past interfere. Now, though, she can't seem to let it go; she's like a dog with a bone."

"You shouldn't refer to your wife as a dog, dad." He doesn't laugh and his eyes fill with the emptiness of minutes ago. I take a sip of my coffee and let the silence grow.

He takes a deep breath and slowly lets it escape through puffed cheeks. "This is hard."

Part of me wants to reach across the table, to take his hands in mine and to tell him things will be okay. But the Ice Queen in me gathers and I sit tight.

"She's asked..." He shakes his head. "She's *told* me I need to let go of my past completely if our marriage is to work; she can't accept me as a new person until there is a line drawn in the sand."

I shrug my shoulders. "And?"

"I've not to speak to you or your sister anymore." He blurts out the sentence and sits back in the faux leather chair. "She wants me to choose: you two or her; my old life, or my new one; the past or the future."

I think about asking him to repeat himself, but it's too dramatic. My mouth opens to speak, but I don't know what to say. Is he joking? No, definitely not. He can't look at me. His jaw quivers. Tears fill his eyes. Questions begin in my mind, but have no endings – hundreds of them. I fold my arms across my chest. "You're serious, aren't you?"

He nods.

"And you've decided to do what she's told you to do?"

His silence is all the answer I need.

"You know Louise won't be able to understand this?"

The light in his blue eyes is dimmer than it used to be; strands of silver look out of place in his short brown hair; the corners of his mouth are starting to turn downwards; and his hands, clasped in front of him, are wrinkled, like those of an old man. I wonder what happened to the man who carried me on his shoulders and chased Ben, Louise and I around the garden.

"You look tired, dad." I stand up; he doesn't move. "You look tired."

I zip my jacket closed and step round the table. In the movies, I would put my hand on his shoulder as I pass, then he would put his hand on mine and we'd stay like that, frozen, capturing the moment for all time. But I simply walk past him and out the cafe door into the early afternoon sunshine. I wince as a gust of wind chills the tears on my cheeks.

13

*S*he awoke to a world of glaring brightness and deafening silence.

Through the thinnest of gaps in her eyelids, the light assaulted her like shards of fire and she blinked rapidly until her eyes adjusted. The sound of her breathing was dull in her ears. Her head felt heavy, like it was coated in concrete. Something inside her told her she should be in excruciating pain, but that medicine eased it away to almost nothing. The taste of blood clung to the back of her throat and the inside of her mouth felt like it was stuffed with cotton wool. She was acutely aware of every single drop of blood as it flowed through her body, gently pinching each nerve-ending as it passed. She smiled inwardly. All her sensations pointed to one thing.

She was alive.

Memories flooded through her as she gained her perspective. She remembered being hit by a car; she saved the boy-pirate, but her body was broken. She remembered being brought to hospital in an ambulance; she wanted to thank the crew for how much they had helped her, but she couldn't quite recall any of their names. She remembered being operated on; somehow, she remembered watching as her heart failed and the doctors brought her back to life. And now, she was awake, waves of brightness blinding her. She tried to move her head to take in her surroundings, but the pain was immediate and severe. She wondered how long she had been unconscious. Closing her eyes again, she drowned in the peace and quiet.

Chapter Thirteen

The waiter approaches us for the third time and asks us if we are ready to order.

"Nearly," my aunt replies, without a glimmer of impatience. "As soon as she gets here, we'll let you know." She takes a sip of her wine, and then under her breath, says "If I don't kill her first."

Adam laughs as he smoothes her hair and kisses her cheek. She leans into him and returns his smile. I haven't seen her as happy since my uncle was alive; she positively glows, hardly able to refrain from beaming with joy in her boyfriend's company. And the best part, the thing that makes me more pleased for her than anything else, is that he is exactly the same as her.

Adam Wilson, thirty-five years old, never married, no children, owns his own home, and business, drives a very, very nice sports car and is utterly gorgeous. That was the description she gave me of him six months ago when she said she had met someone. No one, I told her, could be all those things; there are bound to be one or two skeletons, at least, lurking in his closet. As it turns out, I was wrong – completely wrong.

They had their first date, a blind one organised by a mutual friend, on a dark, rainy Wednesday night in January. By the Saturday of that same week, they had spent every lunch-time, evening and night together. And now, six months later, their relationship has grown to the stage whereby they are almost unable to be apart. Their love for one another was instant and powerful, born of mutual respect, shared interests and unbridled passion, and it remains so today. Their partnership was not one that could ever be attributed to two people looking for something and settling for it in the first person they find. I adore watching them together: the way they move as one; the little smirks and winks they share; the constant, yet not over-the-top affection. He treats her like a princess; he clearly loves her with every bone in his body. And after almost fourteen years of being alone, of living with the ghost of her husband, she has finally got what she deserves.

The three of us wait for only a few moments more before my sister and her boyfriend arrive. They shower us with apologies as they take their seats. Louise seems buoyant. Her cheeks glow pink and her legs bounce the way they have always done when she is excited or happy. She looks at me, grinning from ear to ear. "I don't want to know," I groan, understanding full-well why she is late, and her lips widen even more. Her eyes sparkle with life in the restaurant's lights: a pair of perfectly formed, identical gems, as blue as the morning sky and every bit as innocent. She holds her boyfriend's hand across the table. Something passes between them as they stare into each other. My aunt whispers into Adam's ear and he laughs. Quietly, inwardly, I sigh. Despite being in the company of so much love and so much genuine affection, I feel alone. My thoughts stray to him for the briefest of seconds before the waiter, pleased he can now take our order, rescues me from my memories.

~

After we have eaten, when the sweet tastes of the desserts are beginning to fade from our tongues, we order coffees: Four lattes and an Irish black for Louise. She has already drunk more than a bottle of Chardonnay, and goodness only knows what she had to drink earlier on. I turn to question her, getting as far as "Don't you think…" when she silences me by lifting her hand up to me, palm facing.

"I'm fine," she says, and my aunt and I exchange a look that suggests, perhaps, she is not. There is a strained silence that follows; a second or two of awkwardness before Adam asks to be excused. He makes for the bar, speaking in hushed tones to the staff, before returning looking slightly more pleased with himself than when he left.

A moment later, the waiter appears with our coffees. We watch my sister stir the cream into the dark liquid. "Speaking as the resident alcoholic," she says, spoon in the air, "I'm rather looking forward to this!" Her sideways smile instantly thaws the atmosphere, and she kisses my cheek. Everyone laughs and she whispers to me, "I'm fine, honestly," giving my knee a little squeeze. Conversation resumes, light-hearted and friendly. Louise and Adam share stories and the rest of us laugh. Quickly, the discomfort is forgotten and things are back to normal.

Just before eight o'clock, the alarm sounds from Adam's watch; we all look at one another as he switches it off, and asks for silence. He takes a long drink from his cup, places it on the saucer, and turns to my aunt, reaching for her hand.

"It was here, in this restaurant, six months ago to the day, to the hour and to the minute that I met you," he starts. "And when I saw you, for the only time in my whole life, I knew there was absolutely no doubt. To be truthful, I've never been the romantic sort; I've never subscribed to the 'love at first sight' theory; and until that night I had never really believed love existed, that it was something invented for movies and fairy-tales." I feel Louise press her leg against mine; she feels something building, too. "But you changed all that for me.

You changed my life in a way I could never have imagined possible and for that I am more grateful that you will ever know." He slides his chair back, and produces a small, velvet box from his pocket. Without taking his eyes from hers, he drops down on one knee and opens the box, revealing a diamond ring that catches every sliver of light and radiates it back in dazzling, crisp white. "I love you, with all I am. I can't express it better than that, but it's still not enough. Will you please, please marry me?"

My aunt has both her hands to her cheeks. Her eyes are damp, but her smile is there for everyone to see. She nods her head once. "Of course I will," she says and wraps her arms about his shoulders. I can't move. Louise gasps and grips my arm. I don't remember a time when I have ever been happier for anyone. He slides the ring onto her finger and she beams with joy as she shows off her hand to her nieces.

On cue, the staff Adam spoke to at the bar deliver two bottles of Champagne and pour the five of us a glass each. He raises his in a toast, and we all do the same, repeating as one his single word: "Forever".

~

Six weeks later, we have booked our flights and chosen our dresses. Adam has paid for everything, reminding us it is not our fault he comes from another country. Louise is treating it like a holiday; I remind her we are only away for a week, and it is our aunt's time, not ours, but she doesn't listen. Already, she has promised to find me a man. Adam has two best friends, brothers, and they will be his best men at the ceremony. Louise and I will be bridesmaids for my aunt. In my sister's mind, at least, the numbers all add up.

The three of us (my aunt, Louise and I) sit in a cafe, going through the details of the big day. Our flight leaves in less than a month, but it's clear that between us, everything is already covered. I take a sip of my latte and listen to my sister explain how she "just had to" split with yet another guy. She laughs between sips of her double vodka and coke, reminding us both that Adam was exactly like her until he met my aunt. "I'm waiting on my 'one'," she says, and for a second, in her voice, the Louise from my childhood returns.

To my surprise, as our glasses slowly empty, my aunt mentions our uncle. It's been a long time since I've heard her speak of him, but there is not a day goes by where I don't wish he was still with us. My sister and I remain silent as she says how much she misses him, how much she will always love him and how much she wishes she died with him all those years ago. "But I didn't die," she whispers, and her eyes fix on a space between my sister and me; at a point where the worlds of her past and her future meet. She wears a smile as she says she hopes, wherever he is, he understands and approves. Louise and I agree, and remind her how good Adam is for her, and how good she is for him. We touch our glasses together, and sit in silence for a few moments, each lost in the privacy of our own thoughts.

Louise looks at the remains of our drinks, and offers to get us replacements. Whilst she is at the bar, my aunt quietly asks me what I think of her drinking.

"The only thing that concerns me is how much she can drink without getting drunk," I whisper. "Every time I see her, she has had alcohol, is having alcohol, or is planning to have alcohol. I've tried to talk to her about it, but she is always quick to tell me she's not a little girl anymore."

My aunt nods her agreement. "I spoke to her the night after Adam proposed to me." We watch my sister at the bar, her back to us. "She said she only drinks at the weekend."

Louise empties a shot glass in one swallow, unaware we are watching, and sits it under the counter, out of sight.

"Today is Tuesday," I say. "Does that count?"

She brings the drinks to us on a tray, smiling the smile I have loved for twenty four years. She sets the cups of coffee in front of me and our aunt, and takes a long sip of her vodka through a straw. "What are we talking about?"

"Adam and I have decided to try for a baby."

My aunt's words leap from her mouth like a tiger, and stop Louise and me dead. She smirks and lifts her cup to her lips, blowing on the liquid, looking at us in turn. Her green eyes shine bright over the white porcelain.

"Are you serious?" I ask and she nods. "That's fantastic!"

"You mean we'll be aunties?" Louise asks, gripping my arm. I laugh. So does my aunt. Louise doesn't find it funny. "What? Why are you laughing?"

"Louise, if there is to be a baby it will be our cousin, not our niece."

Her eyes meet mine, her face softens and once again, for a fleeting moment she is my baby sister once more. "You're missing the point." She holds out her hands for us to take, and we do so. She looks from one face to the other, settling on the green eyes. "You may be our aunt in name, but we all know you're more like the biggest sister."

I squeeze both hands and they squeeze back. My little sister is lots of things to me: she is a shoulder to cry on, she makes me laugh and cringe at once with stories of what she gets up to, and she is (especially with her drinking) a constant source of worry. But until this point in our lives, I don't think I have ever been as pleased or as proud as I am now, to call her my very best friend.

14

Gingerly, she tensed and relaxed her fingers. She wiggled her toes. She couldn't see if they were obeying her commands, but it certainly felt like they were. Her breathing was steady, rhythmical, and constant. She licked at her dry lips. They were cracked and raw, and her throat burned.

The room smelled of disinfectant: a sharp, medicinal aroma unique to hospitals. She attempted to speak, but her words caught in her throat. Sleep threatened to consume her, but she knew it was an artificial, dreamless sleep, and she fought to stay awake.

Somewhere off to her right a door opened and padded footsteps crossed the room towards her. A face appeared above her, blurry features in stark contrast to the sterile white ceiling. Her eyes wouldn't focus properly, and she struggled with the effort.

"I see you're awake," the female voice said. "We're glad to have you with us. You gave us all quite a scare earlier on." Her voice was warm and gentle, and it raised and lowered as she spoke like she was singing her words. "Would you like a drink?" A glass of water appeared as if from nowhere and she sipped from the straw. The liquid was cold as it hit her throat and she winced at the feeling. "There, there, now, that's better. I'll let the doctor know you're awake. She'll be along to speak with you shortly." Her tone changed as she said the words; the final sentence sounding sad, almost apologetic. She stood, then, staring at her patient, her eyes speaking words her lips couldn't manage. There was a sudden, heavy silence between them, as if the weight of the world had landed in that tiny room.

The nurse placed a hand on her shoulder, and patted it gently. She let it rest there for a long, long moment.

"And you have a visitor", she continued, the forced smile in her voice betraying her true emotions. "Would you like me to let him in?"

She knew who it was immediately. She needed him here. She needed him now. Tears sprang to her eyes and her breath caught in her throat. It was all she could do to nod.

Chapter Fourteen

From a bench we watch the waves lap the shore, white crowns folding themselves onto the pebbles before being dragged back, exhausted, into the cold blue. Overhead, a weak sun inches its way through a maze of clouds to begin someone else's day, and a light wind lifts cold and salt from the sea, breathing both in our faces. I take a long, slow fill of coastal air and let it soak through my senses for as long as I can. He pulls me closer and I lean into him, resting my head on his shoulder.

"I am very much in love with you," he says, and I know with absolute certainty he means it.

A seagull appears above us, feathers flashing white and silver. It floats in the sky, almost motionless, wings wide, waiting, hoping for us to throw it a few morsels of food; but we have nothing to offer it, and soon it arcs away in search of a meal elsewhere.

"Sometimes, I'd like to be a seagull," he says. I close my eyes and smile. I consider indulging him, letting him speak his wild imagination, but I'm too relaxed. My silence remains and he kisses my hair. "Caw!" he whispers, attempting to mimic a gull, "Caw!"

I lift my head from his shoulder. His eyes are fixed on the horizon, his face deadpan, but he knows I'm watching. "Caw!"

"Robert, stop it," I say, struggling not to laugh. "You're not a seagull, and you're definitely not funny."

He looks at me then, in a way only he has looked at me before; his eyes are filled with such an overwhelming depth of emotion that I feel my heart will stop at any instant. I love this boy so much; I cannot picture my life without him in it. He leans in to kiss me, and I close my eyes as his mouth nears mine. His breath is warm on my skin. And the very instant before our lips touch, he hesitates.

"Caw!" he shrieks, and I jump with fright. He bursts out laughing, and I smack him hard on the arm. I'm trying not to laugh with him, but it's too difficult. His beautiful smile makes it impossible for me to do anything other than join in. I adore the way the shape of his eyes changes when he properly laughs, and the way his cheeks flush pink. Even the sound of his laugh is like nothing I thought could ever exist. Every day, every single day, I am amazed at how much I love him.

He kisses me then, softly, deeply, and my eyes slide shut once more. I feel his smile melt beneath my lips and he lifts his hands to my face, his thumbs stroking my cheeks, his fingers weave into the hair behind my ears. The sea-breeze cools me, the sound of the waves soothes me, and I am floating in the thin air beyond the clouds. I want this to never end; I hope we still kiss as passionately forty years on; I pray he still makes me feel the way I do now until I die.

"Do you love me?" he asks, his voice nothing more than a murmur in my mouth. I nod, continuing to kiss and to dream. "Then tell me."

He lifts his mouth from mine. I remain still, eyes closed, breathing him in, staying lost. I feel his eyes search my face. "I am more in love with you than you can ever know." I pause, waiting for him to say something, but his silence allows me to continue. "You make me believe, Robert, that I am more than I am. You give me hope for the future and when I'm with you, when we are together, I have everything I ever wanted in front of me."

I open my eyes. He is looking at me with a peaceful face, smiling a gentle smile that says he knows something I don't.

"You mean that, don't you?" he asks.

"Of course I do."

"Good," he says standing up and offering me his hand. "Let's take a walk."

Arm in arm, we stroll along the seafront. The gravel pathway crunches with our footsteps, and other than the waves grinding the stones on the shore, it's the only sound. Robert still wears that enigmatic smile of his, and I leave him to his thoughts. Thick, black clouds lumber overhead. The wind is picking up and it's beginning to drizzle; the first few drops of moisture being blown from the sea sting our faces. I quicken the pace – neither of us is dressed for wet weather. The path stretches around a bend where centuries of relentless, pounding waves have carved a small cove. It's isolated, not many people venture this far from the main part of the stony beach, but there is a small shelter there, a wooden frame and roof covering a single bench, and I cross my fingers we are able to reach it before the clouds empty themselves on us.

A low rumble of thunder sounds from the sky at our backs, and Robert and I look at one another, eyes wide. Suddenly, a silent flash of lightning streaks the heavens, and we are running, laughing hysterically, as the rain falls in torrents around us. The light-pink gravel is turned dark-brown within seconds and our feet splash through the puddles, caking our trousers in mud. We turn the corner into the cove and sprint for the shelter as fast as our legs can carry us. Happily, there is no one else there and we throw ourselves under the canopy and onto the bench, breathless and laughing and soaked to our skins.

Robert wipes the water from his face and looks out into the wash of grey. "This is perfect," he says, and rubs his hands together.

"Perfect?" I ask. "We still have to get back to the train station in this!"

He grins at me and raises his eyebrows. "Are you in a hurry?"

"Robert, what's going on? You're acting very strange, even by your standards."

His eyes don't move from mine; he seems to be weighing up something in his mind, taking his time with his thoughts. He does this from time to time, sliding away inside himself, and I search his gaze for a hint of understanding, but find none. The seconds slip by, the rain drums on the roof of our shelter, and it blankets the sea in a heavy, grey mist. I give his hand a little squeeze and stare out at the lost horizon. The wind whips and billows the rain, and it reminds me of when I was a little girl, the net curtain in my mum's kitchen dancing like a snake as the smells of her cooking waft over me. I breathe in through my nose, remembering.

"I want to ask you something." Robert's voice returns me to the present and I blink away the past. He doesn't wait for me to say anything before he continues. "I want you to know how amazing these last seven months have been for me. I want you to know how grateful I am that you chose me to fall in love with, and that you allowed me to do the same with you." He leans into kiss me, and his lips linger longer than usual. The pit of my stomach tingles, and I let out a little moan with the feeling.

"What was that for?" I ask as he separates his mouth from mine.

"Nothing," he whispers. His eyes remain closed. "I just wanted to remember what it was like."

His bottom lip quivers slightly. I've never seen him so nervous. Suddenly, his words start making sense to me, and coupled with his recent odd behaviour, my mind starts racing; my heart feels like a lead weight in my chest. I begin to fear the worst. "What's going on, Robert? Are you okay? What is it you want to ask me?"

He shifts his position slightly, and looks at me with the most intensity I have ever seen. He takes my hands in his.

"Don't worry," he says, acknowledging the panic in my eyes. "It's nothing to worry about – it's just a simple yes or no." Despite his best smile, I don't feel any easier, and I tell him so. His thumbs gently stroke the back of my hands, and he says my name over and over again. The wind whistles around us. Waves rush up the pebbled beach. The sky grumbles in anger, and then flashes once more.

He reaches deep into his pocket and removes a red, velvet box. Confusion lines my forehead; I recognise the box. It is the one I chose for his mum for her birthday. He opens it, revealing the necklace I loved so much.

"I know we're both very young, and neither of us are sure what we want to do with our lives," he starts. I force my eyes from the sparkling jewellery and meet his gaze. "But I want to ask you if you will one day marry me?"

The swing in my emotions is severe. Moments ago, I was expecting him to call things off, or at the very least, slow down a bit. Now, here I am, being proposed to by the boy I love.

"I know it's not a ring," he says, apologetically, offering me the necklace, "but I want it to be our secret. No one need know; not our friends, not our families, no one. Everyone will say we're too young, or too immature, and we will have to justify our decision to the entire world. I don't want this to be stressful for either of us."

I take the necklace in my fingers, letting it dangle. "How long have you been planning this?"

He blushes, and I see a thin film of moisture coat his eyes. "Since I kissed you at the Christmas dance, and felt the absolute certainty that I would one day be with you forever."

I bite the inside of my cheek. I'm definitely not dreaming.

"And it will be our secret?"

He nods and a single tear crawls down his face.

"Then yes," I say, and I kiss the saltwater from his mouth. "Yes, I will one day marry you."

He kisses me back and clips the chain around my neck. Then, and for a long, long time, in the pouring rain and the gusting wind, alone in a little wooden shelter in an ancient cove, my fiancé and I hold each other as if letting go would mean the end of the world.

~

I'm leaving.

His words chase me through the blinding snow, gnawing at my heels as they sink into the thick blanket of white. My legs ache, my lungs burn and the tears that coat my cheeks in silver nip my skin. I'm running as fast as I can, away from him, away from the hurt, but I feel as though I'm standing still. I need to rest; I've been running for almost twenty minutes, flat-out, and I know I cannot go on much longer. The road bends and the snowflakes slide across the air in front of me, now. Ahead, the bridge that links the two sides of my town arches above the freezing river, and my knees lift higher as the drifts deepen.

I don't want to, but I have to. My parents are moving...

I look at my watch. It's almost three o'clock. The streets are deserted; anyone in their right mind is tucked-up in bed, warm and fast asleep. Less than an hour ago, I was getting ready to be one of them, but in the space of a few short sentences my life has been turned upside down.

...away and I'm going with them. I have to. I've tried everything...

Midway across the bridge, I stop. The snow looks black as it passes the pale orange blush of streetlights and I reach out my hand to catch it. Five tiny flakes land on my palm and through my breath I watch them melt into one. I stretch my arm over the railing and the droplet slides into the vast darkness below. There is no sound here; the river is silent; the snow falls in a peaceful hush. I am truly alone.

...but my dad's job, you know? He has to go. Please don't be like that. Do you...

Cold settles on my shoulders; weightless and invisible, yet heavy and tangible. I wrap my arms around my chest to stop myself shivering and on tiptoes, lean out over the railing. Beneath me is another world: A hollow void tumbling into nothing; empty black weaving into empty black; life and light becoming lost in the folds of darkness. I stare at it for a long time, and realise I am staring into the pit of my soul.

...think I want it to be like this? You know how much I love you. I'd do anything...

I stand back and unclip the necklace that has become the symbol of our relationship. It hangs from my fingers, delicate as one of the snowflakes that melt beside it. It still somehow manages to sparkle in the dark, silver and blue, like a star. I fold it into a ball and clasp my fingers around it. My fiancé: I hear his voice echo between the slivers of white that float down from the heavens. He said he loved me; he promised to love me forever; he swore he'd never leave me. And now he has.

...to be with you, for as long as I am alive. And this is killing me, but...

I look at my clenched fist; I feel the metal against my skin. I imagine how it would feel to pull my arm back and throw the necklace, with all my might, over the edge of the bridge, to watch it spiral down into the ether, and to hear the soft splash as it disappears, lost for all eternity in the inky depths of the river below. I bite my bottom lip.

...you have to believe me when I say I will never stop loving you – ever...

I open my fingers. I remember his face, the look in his eyes when he opened the red velvet box and showed me the inside. I knew then he wasn't lying when he said he was in love with me; I still know that now. I close my eyes and put my hand into my pocket. I remove it, empty.

...Don't leave like this. Please? Come back! It's freezing outside. Please, at least...

I turn from the railing and start walking again. Home is fifteen minutes away. In my mind, I hear his voice again, shouting at me as I ran down his street, pleading with me to stop. I begin to cry. Even though we did both tonight, I don't remember the last time we touched, or the last time we kissed; what his lips felt like on mine, or the way he held me. I'm shaking. I'm cold.

...say goodbye. At least let me hear you say it, even just this once!

I run, the snow floating past me like stardust, and I sob uncontrollably. I decide not to see Robert again. He is the love of my life, the one I'm meant to be with forever, and I can't bear the thought of letting him go. If I tell him goodbye, I'll be accepting that we are over, and I cannot allow myself to do that. I know it's wrong; I know there is still a week to go before he leaves, and we could live an entire lifetime in those seven days, but it's better for everyone this way. I stop running and lift my head to the sky. I close my eyes and let the snow fall onto my face.

"We will be together again, Robert. I swear."

My words float upwards, sliding through the cold, dark air. And so, in the painful quiet of a December morning, with the ache of a thousand memories burning through me, I make a decision: I promise to never say goodbye to anyone else until Robert and I are together again.

15

He stood in the doorway, letting his tired eyes adjust to the stark white light of the room. In his hands he carried a bunch of pink roses wrapped in shiny silver foil. He cradled them carefully as he would a child, but all his attention was directed towards the bed.

She laid still, her breathing steady, her swollen eyes closed. He assessed the array of tubes, machines and little bags of fluid, all of which were helping to keep her alive. He watched her for a long moment. His love, his reason for living was ten feet away yet he had never felt so close to her. A thousand memories brushed their velveteen feathers against his skin. He thought of her smile first thing in the morning as she opened her eyes to a new day, and of the way she wrapped her arms around him as they walked, as if letting go would bring death to them both. He thought of how she always smelled like the most perfect summers' afternoon, even after a hard days' work. He thought of her voice the first time she said she was in love with him, her words a whisper almost lost in the breeze. He remembered thinking then, as he was thinking now, that he had never known anything remotely close to happiness until he met her.

He smiled a bittersweet smile. Even here, even now, as she was, she was beautiful.

He was waiting at the hospital for the better part of six hours, arriving as soon as he heard what had happened, but as yet the doctors hadn't told him much of what was going on. That she had been hit by a car was common knowledge, as was the fact she had her brain operated on to relieve pressure from the impact. She was now in the high-dependency ward. Other bits and pieces of information were obtained from staff as they worked their rounds. He was sure he had a fair picture painted by the time he opened the door to her room.

The nurse who came to get him had warned of the sight that would greet him: the tubes and electronic monitors and bandages were all perfectly normal – nothing to worry about, she said. She told him they had stabilised her, but she was to remain where she was for continued observation. He breathed deeply. He prayed she would be all right.

The foil wrapper rustled and she stirred. He stood where he was, waiting for her to see him. She licked at her lips and blinked her eyes open. Slowly, as he waited, unmoving in the silence, she turned her head to face him.

And she smiled.

Chapter Fifteen

"Take your marks!"

Hands shoulder-width apart, I place my thumbs and index fingers on the grass and settle down on one knee. To my right, the other eleven girls of my class do the same. I stare at the ground, at a single white daisy that momentarily sits in my shadow, and I concentrate. A cool breeze blows on the back of my neck.

"Get set!"

I rise up, keeping my fingers on the verge of the painted white line, poised to run at the next sound. A few loose strands of my hair hang down, long spirals that gleam light-amber in the early afternoon sunshine. A hush descends on the crowd of parents and friends. I imagine my mum yelling for joy as I'm first to break the thin strand of ribbon that waits at the finish.

"Go!"

I push off hard, remembering what my mum said, and look for the finish line. I force my arms to work, driving my eight-year-old legs as fast as they can. "Quick, short steps," she said, "like a baby." A hundred metres isn't that far. My feet pound into the grass. From either side of the makeshift track, cheers of encouragement ring out. I listen for my name, but it's too noisy to separate one voice from another. My friend Joanne starts to pull away from me, and I grit my teeth, chasing her. But with every breath, she gets further ahead and within seconds I am looking at the back of her white polo shirt. Around about half distance, I glance across to my right and see a long ragged line of white.

There is no one behind me. I'm last.

I push as much as I can, forcing my legs to move faster. The crowd cheers, spurring me forward. There is a burning sensation in my chest. Joanne runs further ahead. The other girls do too.

Last night, at dinner, my dad told me it was the taking part and having fun that was important, but afterwards, when I was in bed, my mum came in and told me she was a schools champion sprinter. Her eyes glowed with happiness as she told me stories of her success and of her most memorable wins. She said she knew I could come in first if I simply put my mind to it. I told her it was just a sports day, that it wasn't a competition. But, sitting on the end of my bed, her eyes dark and tired, her voice a distant whisper, she told me everything in life is a competition; if you're not going to win it, why bother? For a second, just before she left me alone in the dark, she leaned in towards me and I thought she was going to kiss me goodnight. But even though she didn't, even though she was only wiping some fluff from my pillow, I fell asleep grateful for the chance to make her love me just a little bit more.

I grit my teeth. Every breath feels like fire. I run as fast as I can, but I know it's not fast enough. I picture my mum's face, her disappointment clear, as out of all the children, hers comes in last. The distance between me and the other girls grows, and I know I won't catch them.

A cheer erupts from the crowd and the broken ribbon flutters to the ground as Joanne raises her arms in victory. I keep running, baby-steps like my mum said. To generous applause, I cross the finish line dead last. Even though I have never been good at sports, even though I didn't really expect to do well, I desperately wanted to win for my mum; I wanted her to be proud of me.

Joanne gives me a hug. Her cheeks are scarlet and she's out of breath. In her hand, she holds a gold-coloured rosette, with '1$^{st'}$ emblazoned in purple. She skips away, beaming with joy, into the outstretched arms of her parents.

My breath returns to normal as I wander around looking for my mum. A horn sounds from the car park, and I see her standing by the driver's door. The engine is already running, and as I walk across to her, she climbs inside and slams the door shut. I feel as though a dark cloud has blotted the sun. With a heavy heart I sit on the seat beside her and she drives off before I even have the chance to clip my belt.

"Did you see the race?" I force a smile. "Joanne..."

"Don't!" she shouts, and tiny balls of spit jump from her mouth onto the windscreen. She points a finger at me, and grimaces as though she is in a lot of pain. "Just don't."

We journey home in thick silence. I think of ways to say I tried my hardest, for her. I want her to know I would've done anything to win, but I'm just not that good at running. I want to hear her say she is proud of me for doing my best anyway. But the drive ends before any more words are spoken and my mum stalks into the house, leaving me alone with my failure and the all too familiar stream of tears glisten on my cheeks.

~

"Are you ready?" the instructor shouts in my ear, his voice barely audible above the howl of wind and the drone of the engine.

"Ready!"

Eighteen thousand feet below, through a thin veil of cotton-white clouds, the landscape shimmers like an image from a dream. Ahead, the horizon is a dark blue arc that stretches across forever and higher still, the sun is a perfect circle of silver in a flawless sheer of sky.

I'm surprisingly calm as the command to lean forwards is given; my breathing is slow and controlled, and I don't feel my heart beat any faster than normal. I grip the handles either side of the open door and stand with the balls of my feet on the edge. Infinity beckons.

"On three!" he shouts. "Then pull us out! Remember to keep your head back, your knees bent and your arms forward!"

I nod my understanding. A smile crosses my lips. The fulfilment of a life-long ambition stares me in the face, and I'm doing it on the most perfect day in the most perfect location. I wonder what Louise is thinking as she waits for me on the ground.

"Three!"

With a deep breath, the aeroplane leaves my feet and I'm falling. The air rushes by at a speed I've never known before; my cheeks billow like sails; a scream of joy pierces the deafening roar in my ears and I realise it comes from my throat. I can't remember the last time I smiled like this. I think I might burst.

A single word wraps its arms around me: Freedom.

This is what it feels like to be completely free. For the next thirty seconds or so, before the parachute deploys and before I will gently glide to earth, nothing matters – absolutely nothing. My mind empties of everything. This is joy in its purest form. This is what life should feel like.

The altimeter on my wrist reads twelve thousand feet. Two thousand feet to fall before the canopy opens. It amazes me how I can breathe normally with the force of the air buffeting my face.

I remember, on a school trip, a teacher telling a group of us that you have space in your brain for thousands upon thousands of memories and you can call upon any one of them, at any given time. But she then said that there are the special ones you keep in a secret place; the twenty or so memories that define you, which you will hear echo in the final beat of your heart. What's just happened to me in the last minute and a half of my life will definitely be one of those.

The instructor taps my shoulder. It's time.

I close my eyes, locking in the memory, capturing my every sense. I'm falling, happy and free, at peace with myself for the first time in years.

And I know a part of me will be falling forever.

~

Two weeks before my seventh birthday, we move house. Louise and I are getting too old to share a room, my mum says, and so we cross the river, to a brand new house with space enough for everyone, and a huge garden at the back for Ben to run around in.

My parents promise me a double-bed in exchange for getting rid of most of the toys and games that clutter the floor and fill the cupboards of my old room. They give me a box that barely reaches my knees and tell me that whatever I can fit into it, I can keep – the rest will either go to charity or be thrown away. And so I do what they ask, the thought of being able to lie star-shaped on my new giant mattress as I fall asleep each night is at the front of my mind as I choose the ten or so items that I will take from one stage of my life into the next.

We move to our new house on a Friday. My bedroom, with its' huge, brand new bed, brand new wardrobe, brand new chest of drawers and lonely box of old toys looks out over the front garden; my sister's room, smaller and crammed full with everything from the old place, has a great view of the woods and fields at the back of the house. For the first time in memory, Louise and I are eager to get to our beds; even on holiday or when we stay at our aunt's house, we have to share a room or a bed, and for me, the prospect of not hearing her act out her dreams is wonderful.

But during the night, I'm woken by her pushing at my shoulder, sobbing.

"There's a ghost," she whispers between shallow breaths.

I switch on my bedside lamp. It's clear she's been upset for a while: Her cheeks are blotchy and soaking wet and her entire body trembles. She stands with her arms at her sides, the cuffs of her pink pyjamas dark with wiped tears. Her thumb is hidden between her lips. I lift up my duvet and she climbs in beside me. With an arm wrapped round her, I listen to her cry the last of her fear away in short sniffs.

"Shall we go and see if the ghost is away?"

She shakes her head.

"You need to go back to your own bed, Louise. I'll tell you what – you lie here, nice and warm, and I'll take a quick look. Okay?"

Without letting her respond, I slide out of bed and sneak along the corridor, from my room into hers, careful not to waken anyone else.

I wait in the eerie blue half-light for my eyes to adjust.

Her bed faces the window. Outside, a full moon glows pale yellow in the black sky, and it shines through swaying trees to cast liquid shadows on the wall to my left: Her ghost. A soft smile plays on my lips. To be fair to her, in a strange house, sleeping on her own for the first time, I can understand why she is so scared. But as there are no curtains or blinds to block out the nightmare, I'm at a loss as to what to do to help her.

And then, in spite of what it will mean for me, I have an idea.

I tiptoe back to my room. She is sitting up on my bed, knees to her chin, big blue eyes wide open and her arms wrapped around her shins.

"Is it still there?" she asks in the smallest voice. "Did you see it, too?"

I say nothing, but walk to the box at the end of my bed and open it. I lift from it my stripy-pyjama panda bear and lie down beside my sister.

"When I was your age," I start, "I was scared of everything: Ghosts, goblins, witches, vampires – the lot. But do you know what I was afraid of the most?" She shakes her head, wet eyes staring at me expectantly. "The dark; I was terrified of it! I was so scared that I couldn't even get to sleep at night in case something came to get me!" I give her the biggest smile I can, and she almost manages one in return. "And then, one day, I got him."

I pass her my panda. As she takes it from me, I feel part of my childhood slip from my fingers. She clutches it to her chest.

"He'll protect you, just as he did me. And if you listen really carefully, sometimes you can even hear him speak." She looks at me in disbelief. I shrug my shoulders. "If you don't think it's true, he won't be able to save you."

She frowns, saying nothing. For a long moment, the two simply stare at each other. Then she puts his mouth to her ear and nods once.

"He'll help you sleep."

Louise looks at me as though I'm an idiot. "I know!" she says. "He's just told me!"

Holding hands, we walk quietly to her room and I tuck her in. The three of us sit together for a while and watch the shadows from the trees outside dance on the wall. Eventually, she yawns and smacks her tired lips together.

"Night night," she says, her eyes slipping closed. She hugs her new best friend close to her chest as sleep takes her. I lean in to kiss her forehead. It's a long time before I leave, and as I watch her drift into a world of dreams, I smile.

My little sister: I just can't believe how much I love her.

16

When the nurse left her she drifted back to sleep, too weak to fight the anaesthetic. She slept a shallow, dreamless sleep – if sleep it was – and awoke to the thought she had missed him. It felt like a hole had opened up somewhere inside, a chasm that threatened to suddenly consume her. She bit her bottom lip. She so desperately wanted to see him, to apologise, to tell him how much she loved him and to hear him say the same to her. She wanted to feel his hand in hers, the familiar touch lending more comfort and reassurance than words ever could. And she wanted to look into his eyes, to see in their bright green an even brighter future.

She immediately thought of the card, the one she had written after her appointment; the card that would explain to him her news in a way she never could. She wondered what became of it.

Then she heard a rustle of paper across to her right, where the door was. She blinked her eyes to make sure she was still awake, and carefully turned her head. When she saw him stood waiting in the doorway, felt his warm eyes filling her with hope, all the pain and trauma, uncertainty and fear that burned inside her vanished.

And she smiled at him with all she was.

Chapter Sixteen

Seven years ago, my little sister and I sat in this very office and listened to the consultant gynaecologist deliver the death-blow to my chances of ever being a biological mother. But today, with the memory of history burning like coals behind my eyes, I'm here hoping to be told something else that will change my life forever.

The room hasn't changed. Waves of cinnamon still waft periodically from a little plug-in freshener, and a thin net-curtain weaves and ripples with the heat from the radiator beneath the window. Photographs of his family, grandchild now included, still occupy one side of his desk, and the complicated telephone and bulky computer monitor have been replaced with a sleek handset and a white, ultra-slim flat screen.

The door opens and my doctor steps into his office, carrying a single brown paper folder. He catches me staring at it, and pats it gently.

"Thank you for coming in at such short notice. I thought we'd better have a chat as soon as I got the results. So, how are you feeling?" he asks as he backs into his leather chair. Long fingers spell out an answer to something on the keyboard.

"I'm doing fine, thanks."

"And what about tonight – will you be joining in with the festivities? Any fancy-dress parties lined up?"

I shake my head. "Halloween and I have never agreed.

Even when I was little, dressing up as a clown or as a fairy or as... I don't know... a dice was completely foreign to me. Everyone seemed to get so stressed!"

"Well, my daughter Sophie – you know Sophie, don't you? – is taking my grandson out for the first time tonight." He stops typing, takes off his glasses and opens the folder. "He's beside himself with excitement. They've spent hours on his costume, hours; the boy has been driving his poor mother round the twist!"

I smile. "If she knocks on my door, I'll be sure to give him lots of treats. What is he dressing up as?"

"A pirate," he says. His finger taps a single sheet of paper in front of him, and his face breaks into a grin. "Now, enough of this chit-chat; how would you like to hear some good news for a change?"

~

His words still ring in my ears as I glide down the corridor. The letter, typed perfectly on crisp white headed paper, sits in my bag, a silent testament to my condition. His signature is scratched on the bottom, a scrawl above his name and title. It's official. Nothing can change the truth now.

The nurses and patients smile at me as I pass; my mood seems to spread from one face to the next. I wonder if they can tell what's going on inside of me. I whisper my condition over and over again. It feels like tiny bubbles of pure joy fizz and pop against every nerve in my body. Things are so much clearer now: Colours are richer, edges smoother; the harsh surface of reality has become a playground's spongy floor. I have plunged headfirst into a watercolour painting and I'm drowning. I love it.

The automatic doors slide open, and I skip out into the cold. Already, the world is crawling under the cover of darkness, whispering for us all to go home, to be with our friends and families. The night promises to be cold and frosty, the sky pinpricked with a handful of stars. I remember my aunt's words as I stare into the heavens, remembering their meanings to me over the years. If my smile could grow any wider, it would.

As I cross the car park, heading for the main road, a thought occurs to me, and I stop walking. Under the pale white glow of a light as round as the moon, with my breath swirling to nothing in the air before me, it dawns that as soon as I tell anyone the news, my life will never be the same again. Everything will change, for the better, certainly, but it will be completely different. These moments, these few hours until I tell Robert, will be the last of me as I know it.

Robert. My heart beats faster when I think of him. I imagine his reaction, his grey eyes flaming to life, his smile swallowing up the world. It's the one thing he wanted; the one thing that could have driven a wedge between us had he not been so wonderful. With anyone else, I'm sure the relationship wouldn't have lasted.

"Are you all right?" a woman asks as she passes me, and I realise I am slumped against the lamppost, no doubt looking dazed and confused as a thousand thoughts chase through my mind.

"Oh, I'm fine!" I say as I stand upright and smile apologetically. She nods as she walks away from me, into the gloom. And to no one except myself, I add, "I'm just trying to work out how to tell my boyfriend something."

~

The bus is late. A small crowd gathers waiting with me, oblivious to my joy. I smile at them with each accidental eye-contact, and they return the gesture, some finding it easier to do so than others. I still wrestle with my thoughts, still struggle with the enormity of how our lives will change and then the cold starts to bite. It nips my cheeks like tiny crab's claws and I pull white woollen gloves over my fingers to stop them hurting. A thin sheen of frost has formed already on the Perspex shelter, and patches of silver coat grass verges. I put my matching hat on, too. Half-heartedly, I curse Robert for taking the car to work today. But I couldn't tell him why I was coming here. He doesn't even know there's the slightest possibility...

On the bus, with shadowy billboards blurring past through clouded windows, and strangers ignoring one another with practised unity, I decide to make him dinner. Like an evil Halloween witch, I cackle inwardly at the genius of my plan. I never cook for him, unless it's a really special occasion; this way he will know something is going on and hopefully it will make my job a little bit easier. I get off a few stops before I should and float in to the supermarket on my new-found sense of joy.

With the basket full of steak, potatoes, frozen cheesecake and a bottle of the Californian red wine he loves so much, I stand in line at the checkout. The doctor's words still swim through me – if only I could tell Robert in the same beautiful way he told me. And then, like lightning, inspiration strikes.

I leave the checkout and hurry past the long aisles of washing powder, pet foods, furniture polish and deodorants. Next to the main entrance, with the decimated remains of the Halloween display behind me and my basket at my feet, I stand with my hands on my belly and stare at the array of greetings cards.

I don't want one that telegraphs the message, nor do I want one that makes light of the situation, so for a long time, I scan the selection from top to bottom, mentally eliminating each card as my eyes pass over them.

And then, tucked in behind a twenty-first birthday card, totally out of place, I find it. Six inches long and four across, with pale, pastel blue colours at the top darkening through the spectrum to the deepest shades at the bottom. Two cute cartoon bears sit on a bench, hand in hand and a single word is printed above the pair. The word is 'Forever'.

Another layer of excitement falls gently into place, on top of the happiness and the joy and the sense of utter completeness. With the blue card and its mauve envelope in my basket, I rejoin the line and pay for the groceries, my smile spreading to the lips of the checkout operator, who winks at me as I leave. I glow; I know I do.

There's a small cafe in the supermarket, and I order a coffee and settle down at a table. It takes six words to change someone's life, and I carefully write them on the cards' blank insides. The letter from the doctor is folded one more time and I close the card around it, and seal the envelope shut. Again, I play out the scene in my imagination as he opens it: his initial suspicion at coming home to a cooked meal; his confusion as I slip the envelope across the table to him, my silence adding to the moment; his disbelief as my history – our history – unravels before his eyes; and then his pure, raw, naked joy. I feel my cheeks redden at the thought of how little sleep we will get tonight.

I head back out into the cold and the dark and the icy pavements. The carrier bags, one in each hand, aren't that heavy and I decide to walk the couple of miles back home. The air is bitter, but it's clean and crisp and it seems only to add to my excitement. I whistle as I walk, and it's after a few hundred yards that I realise I'm whistling the tune Robert and I first danced to. I remember that night as though it were yesterday; I don't think there has been a day in the last fifteen years when I haven't thought of it or of him. My smile grows.

Robert; my beautiful, beautiful Robert; what I would give to be holding you right now.

17

They held hands for a long time before either said anything. No words, it seemed, were immediately necessary and the silence that sat between them was comfortable and warm. A soft breeze brushed at the space between them, fanned by a heating vent in the ceiling. The net curtain shifted slightly. A steady flicker of green light ticked from a monitor to her left; the monotonous beep of the heart monitor turned off. There was muted sound of activity from the corridor outside, but inside the room, time had ceased to matter.

His fingers delicately stroked the bare skin of her forearm. He stared at her, stared past the bandages and swollen eyes, past the cuts and bruises, and knew he was looking at the woman he loved more than anything else in the world.

She breathed in the gentle waves of his aftershave, a fond, subtle scent that remained distinct in the wash of the sharp, bleach-like hospital smell. Her eyes were getting used to the light in the room. She found his eyes burning through her, and she was soothed by their intensity. Everything, she thought to herself, would be all right.

She opened her mouth to speak but the words remained in her bone-dry throat. He hushed her, smiling as he did, and she stopped trying.

"Hey you," he whispered, his voice sounding more beautiful than she could ever remember. "Have you been playing in the traffic again?"

Chapter Seventeen

My eyes slide open and the memory leaves me; a softer darkness fills my eyes. The alarm clock reads zero two seventeen. I prop myself up on my pillows and watch the shadows unfold in the half-light. I call it a memory, even though it's not – It can't be; I haven't yet lived it. It's a dream, one I've been having since before I can remember. It teases me, flirting on the edge of a nightmare, like a lone infant bouncing a ball at the side of a busy road. It surfaces again and I let it weave through me.

I am on the shore, white sand under my feet, green leaves overhead and a low, yellow sun on the horizon. A buzz surrounds me, a steady hum like a swarm of insects singing at once, but I am not troubled by it. Someone – I can't see who – stands by my side, holding my hand. There's a warm breeze that blows from a windless sky. And then my mum appears. She is standing in front of me, on a flat barge, staring, with her hands at her sides. Under no power or control, the barge begins to move, slipping into the distance, taking her with it, taking her away from me. I try to speak, but can't. I want to shout out to her, but something invisible covers my mouth. I feel the weight of my years pin me to the floor. I have to break free from this. I must...

~

I park my car under the branches of a huge Oak tree, listening as the last of the rain drips from its leaves and lands in heavy splashes on the roof and windscreen. I'm a good bit early, but I step out into the fresh, spring air to wait nonetheless. With the clouds rinsed dry, the sky is puffy and white, and the same wind that carries the scents of the park over me, gently blows patches of powder blue into view. I rub my hands together, nervously.

My mum called a couple of nights ago, asking me to meet her here. "It will just be the two of us," she said. As usual, there was little conversation surrounding the point of the call, her words carefully chosen to limit the need for prolonging a process neither of us was comfortable with. But in the last thing she said before she hung up, her voice softened, and sounding like I've never heard her before she whispered, "Don't say anything to your sister, please."

That's why I'm so nervous. That's why I had my dream last night.

I stroll around the car park, waiting, my mind swimming with possibilities of why she wants to meet. Birds peck the damp grass in search of food; a young couple, still hooded against the now-absent rain, stroll back to their car having walked the circuitous route arm-in-arm; and a helicopter floats in the sky, invisible to me beyond the huge trees. The world spins in time with my thoughts, unaware.

She arrives, her car crunching to a stop on the gravel, just as the sun breaks free from the clouds and beams strands of translucent honey through branches of infant leaves. Her eyes sparkle with her approach and for a moment, as we stand less than two feet apart, I think she is going to hug me. Instead, she lifts her hand to my arm and rubs it at the elbow.

"You look great," she says. Her smile is warm and genuine, and I return it.

"Thanks mum. You don't look so bad yourself." I'm not

lying. Right now, she could pass for my older sister – she does not look anywhere near her thirty-nine years. Her skin is smooth, like Louise's, and since she split with my dad the dark grey bags under her eyes have vanished. The brown clip in her shoulder-length hair matches her knee-high boots, into which she's tucked her jeans. And she completes the look of a catalogue model with a beautiful deep-red, over-sized knitted sweater.

"I used to come here when I was pregnant with you," she says as she leads us onto the path. "And I managed to come once or twice after you were born, but because we didn't have a car, and, well, you know…"

"You've never told me that before," I say.

"There are lots of things I've not told you." Her tone hints at an apology, and I feel her search my face. "And lots of things I have, I wish I didn't."

We continue on the path. I let the silence settle once more before speaking again. "I do love this walk, though. I've always felt safe here, like I belong."

Our steps are in unison and she walks now with her eyes closed, head lifted to the sun.

"Are you going to…" is as far as I get before she gently hushes me by raising a finger to her mouth.

"Let's just enjoy this for a while, okay?" Her smile is not one I have ever seen on her before. Her face is cast in amber. "There's plenty of time to talk about things. Besides, when did we last do anything like this?"

I snort. "When did we ever?"

"Exactly," she says, still walking without looking.

And then the strangest thing: She links her arm around mine.

My insides wilt. I can't recall the last time she properly touched me, never mind showed me any affection. She seems to read my mind and gives a reassuring little squeeze. I cast a sideways glance, but her expression hasn't changed; mine has, though – there is a certain kind of smirk on my lips that I know has never been there before.

For the next ten minutes or so, the silence between us remains; but it is peaceful, like a delicate shroud around our shoulders, not strained or awkward like it usually is. A squirrel scampers up a tree and out of sight as we approach. Bees drift from bud to bud, aware of nothing besides their purpose. Something chirps its song from the arching labyrinth of wood and leaves overhead.

"I used to tell you, when you were very, very little, that pandas lived in these woods." Her words are just above a whisper, like she is scared someone hears us. "Do you remember?"

I shake my head.

"That's why we bought you that panda with the stripy pyjamas."

"The one I gave to my sister?"

"The very one. Your father made up a story of how the fairies needed a special girl to look after a brand new baby panda-cub, and you said you'd take care of him forever. And then, as you say, you gave it to Louise."

The ground beneath our feet is spongy and moist with the earlier rain.

"Do you know why she ended up with the bear?" I ask, careful to match steps.

"I do," my mum says after a short silence, "I do. And it broke my heart how proud I was of you for looking after your sister like that."

Her confession startles me. Nothing could have prepared me for such a statement, and I almost stop to ask her to repeat herself. But she marches on, guiding me forwards. Again, she knows my thoughts.

"I'm sorry I have never told you how very proud I am of you. You have every right not to trust me or even like me." She leads us towards a bench and we sit down.

That's twice in the space of a few minutes I've been stunned by her. Even if I wanted to, I couldn't speak. My mum is proud of me.

She groans, and leans back on the bench. "What must I have been like for you? I mean, how much did I ruin your childhood?" Her questions float into the sky, and she doesn't wait for an answer, as though any response from me just now would simply be an intrusion. "It wasn't deliberate, you know. I didn't mean to be so unkind to you. God, you must have detested me all those years! What the hell was I doing?" She still hasn't looked at me, and a single thought fights its way to the front of my mind. "What a waste," she says, almost speaking to herself. "What a waste."

"Are you dying, mum?" The question is out before I can stop it. She turns to me, eyes wide; something passes over her face: a flicker, a shadow. A smile grows, and then fades. Her eyes close, and she fills her lungs with a deep, deep breath. When she looks at me again, her eyes are damp.

"Is that how bad things are? Is this how awful I've let our relationship become?" She shakes her head, a subtle movement that is almost lost to me. "My girl, my beautiful, baby girl – have I honestly let things get so far gone that when we finally speak properly, you think I'm dying?"

"So you're not dying, then?"

Our eyes meet and at the exact same moment, we both laugh aloud; for a long minute, it's the only sound, and it echoes through the trees around us. As it subsides, leaving us alone once more, I feel closer to my mum than ever. Her cheeks glisten with a mixture of tears. Carefully, hesitantly, she rests her hand on my knee.

"There's so much I want to tell you; so much I want you to understand before we leave here today." She winks at me and pats my leg. "And no, I'm not dying! Come on, let's walk for a while. I think I've got some explaining to do."

~

A little over twelve weeks later, I'm at the airport. My sister, ashen-faced and moody, leans on a pillar beside me; our mum is at the check-in desk, heaving the last of her bags onto the belt.

"I can't believe the day is finally here," Louise sighs. I hold my hand out for her to take, and she links fingers.

The day Louise is talking about, today, is the day my mother emigrates.

Since the divorce, she has become a new woman: vibrant, passionate, decisive, and adventurous, and the decision to leave was a simple one. Louise has university to go to anyway, and she will live in my spare room when she is not on campus. Now, with the confidence of a teenager, our mum strides towards us, sunglasses perched on top of her head, a wicker handbag over her shoulder and beaded jewellery clicking.

"We've got time for a coffee," she says, and together, with her arms wrapped around us, we march through the terminal building.

Her flight leaves in three hours, and we spend as much of that time as possible telling stories and reminiscing of our childhood: three different points of view on the exact same event; a new page of understanding turned with every sentence heard.

Eventually, the final call is announced over the loudspeakers. An invisible weight descends on us and, looking away, my sister wipes at her eyes. My throat tingles; I bite at my lip to stop it trembling. Our mum takes both our hands.

"This is lovely," she says. "I couldn't have wished for this to be any more perfect."

I know she's right.

Louise stands and forces a smile. "Come on, let's get you on the plane – this is getting far too sentimental for the ice-queen here! She might actually melt."

Just before the security check-point, under a hanging basket overflowing with green leaves, my mum turns to face us both.

"I need you to stay here," she says. Her eyes shine with tears. "This is hard enough as it is. She hugs my sister and holds her for a long, long time. Strands of saltwater stream down my cheeks; I look at the floor, through the haze, and kick at the white tiles.

"Who would have thought you'd be sad to see me go?" She has her arms around me, her mouth by my ear. Louise is breaking her heart, sobbing like she was a child once more. "I am so, so sorry I wasn't there for you," she whispers. "I was wrong, and I need you to know there has never been a mother more proud of their child as I am of you. I love you. I love you with more than I am." She squeezes me tightly; I don't want her to let go. Even if I wanted to say something in return, I couldn't. "Thank you for giving me the chance to get to know you properly these last few months. Thank you."

She steps back.

My little sister buries her head into my shoulder. She moans, breaths ragged, and I hold her. A breeze from the air-conditioning unit nearby chills my tears, and I wipe them away.

"Goodbye for now, my beautiful girls," our mum says as she picks up her bag and slips the glasses over her eyes. Her words mingle with the buzz of the countless other passengers. "I love you both!"

"Bye, mum," Louise cries. I won't say it. I won't.

Still facing us, she steps onto the long conveyor belt that takes the passengers down to security and to the gates beyond. Above her, a huge billboard shows a perfect yellow sun on the horizon. Louise takes my hand in hers and we watch as our mum slowly slides away from us.

I remember this: The white floor; the green leaves; the sun on the horizon; the cooling breeze; the buzz in my ears; my mum... I remember this: It's my dream.

My throat tightens; my mouth clamps shut. The words are there, waiting to escape, but I'm gagged by twenty-one years of hurt. Three months is nowhere near long enough to make right the damage she did to me, but I want her to know how I feel. I've never told her and I may never get another chance. Conflict rages within. My mouth is dry. She doesn't deserve to hear me say it; she doesn't deserve...

"I love you, mum!" I shout at the top of my voice.

The words are out before I can stop them; the sense of release is overwhelming, and my emotions overflow like champagne from a shaken bottle. She waves with both hands, blowing us kisses and smiling as big a smile as I've ever seen.

"I love you, mum!" Louise shouts.

"I love you!"

And bouncing on tiptoes, with my dream – my memory – dissolving before my watery eyes, we wave until she has slid from view.

18

What little conversation they could manage was light. He was doing his best to keep her spirits high, and she was letting him. They avoided talk of her injuries, partly because it was too painful for them to discuss, partly because neither of them really knew what they were. Her head was heavily bandaged, her eyes swollen and red, her lips bloodless and grey. That her legs were broken was obvious – she almost managed to laugh when he offered to sign each cast – but other than the bumps, scrapes and bruises, there was no indication of why she was still in isolation.

They were alone for only a few minutes when the door opened. The doctor who entered smiled warmly as she introduced herself, her shoulder-length auburn hair tied back in a pony-tail revealing a delicate, surprisingly youthful face. Hazel eyes studied each of them for a moment, high cheekbones dusted pink. She stood at the end of the bed, her arms folded across the lemon blouse she wore, stethoscope around her neck. An identity card was clipped to the front pocket of her dark-blue trousers. She started to speak, but stopped, the smile gone from her lips. She stared at the floor. Her hesitancy made him sit up, worry etched on his face.

"What's wrong?" he asked. He reached for his lover's hand and squeezed gently.

"I'm afraid," she began, "I have some bad news."

Chapter Eighteen

Thick, heavy clouds rumble overhead, varying shades of dark on the night sky, and the silent wind that drives them tugs at my shoulders, pushing me, pulling me – daring me to jump.

I take a look over the edge once more and stare down at the inky black. The river, beckoning two hundred feet below, is like a bottomless chasm; if I fall, I'll be falling forever. I wouldn't want it to be like that. Cold metal bites at my fingers as my grip tightens. I close my eyes for a second or two, breathing slowly, breathing calmly. I step back. The steady drum of heartbeat in my ears is the only sound.

Sunrise will be at half past four, still a good twenty minutes away, but already the horizon is burning silver. A tight smile crosses my lips. Last night, despite a day of torrential rain, the clouds made way for a wonderful sunset; I stood on the other side of this very bridge, watching it sink, liquid-gold into black, painting the pebbled sky in rose-pink and honey. It was, I decided, to be my last. And it was, I decided, fate that allowed me see it as beautiful.

It was my last sunset; this morning is my last sunrise; today will be my last day on earth.

Twenty-three years and four days have passed since I cried my way into the world; twenty-three years of emptiness and of loneliness, of hurt and of rejection. I can't take any more. The apathy that swells within me eats my soul like a cancer and I'm no longer able to control it. I need to leave, to let go, to accept I don't belong. I have friends, I have family, yet I feel as anonymous as a raindrop in a thunderstorm or a blade of grass on a meadow. On reflection, the decision to take my own life was a simple one – I'm only surprised I didn't make it earlier.

A splash of amber crowns the distant skyline and the world becomes a shadow of itself. I lean on the railing at my back and watch the light creep slowly toward me, timeless, perpetual. Any other day, this would be a sunrise merely worthy of a glance, of nothing more than a moment's appreciation: It is not special in any way; it is not influenced by some rare astronomical event; it doesn't even merit a camera to capture it forever. But when it is to be your last – as it is when anything is to be your last – it adopts an entirely different meaning.

I wait, patient, still, until the sun has risen too high for me to look at it any longer. The image is burned in my mind and I blink away the black spots on my eyes. And as I begin the long walk home, I nod, answering the question that is being asked from somewhere deep inside: Are you sure? Are you sure?

~

The face in the mirror stares back at me, eyes soft and dark and empty of hope; tired eyes, lonely eyes, eyes that have lost purpose and direction; eyes that reflect a world of sorrow and a life of self-pity.

I lift my hand to it and touch the cold glass, running my fingers down the image. There used to be such promise there, such passion. Where, I wonder, has it gone?

On the dressing table, cleared of the usual array of perfumes, make-up, cleansers and tissues, sit seven creamy-white envelopes. Each one has been given a name, written cleanly and carefully on the front. And each one lies empty for the time being, waiting for me to find the right words.

The afternoon is young when I begin the task of saying the things I have always wanted to, to those few who have meant something in my life. I keep each note brief: eight or ten lines; no questions; no uncertainty; nothing left unsaid. It's a surprisingly simple task. When consequence is removed, when there will be no repercussions of the contents, truth and honesty flow freely. I devote as much time as I can to each and every word, aware they will be my testament – aware they will be all that remains of me.

Two of the seven envelopes will remain sealed forever. One is for my uncle, for his memory and for his influence on my life during the twelve years I knew him. I didn't get the chance to tell him just how much I loved him, how much he helped me understand things, and there has not been a day since his death I have not wished for the chance to do so.

The other, is for my mum.

~

As evening approaches, as the world outside rushes home from work, I prepare for the end. I wipe down the kitchen surfaces, vacuum, tidy away all the clutter in my living room and fold all my clothes away neatly. I'm surprisingly calm, resigned to my fate as I go about the chores, the question from earlier becoming less and less frequent in my mind. I twist the taps on the bath, pour in a capful of bubble-bath, light some tea-candles, and barefoot, wander the rooms of my home. The sound of water splashing on water follows me.

I sit on the edge of my bed and wonder what I have done to deserve this life? Everything I have ever wanted has been denied to me; my dreams lay in tatters, scattered behind me, the letter from my doctor telling me I'll never be able to conceive. Anger swells within, a familiar sense of injustice that has plagued me since I can remember. It fills my chest like liquid lead, and I curse. If I could cry, I would. My arms wrap instinctively around my stomach, and I gently rock back and forth, back and forth, until the pain subsides.

The bathroom in my flat doesn't have a window, and with the door closed I am in my own little dimly-lit tomb. Shadows dance on the tiled walls in fluid waves of gold and amber. The air is warm and sticky. My clothes are folded into a neat pile and the cordless phone is on the floor next to the bath, tucked into a towel in case it gets damp. I smile. Even now, I'm worried about the tiniest of details. The water is a perfect temperature and a perfect depth, and I slide in up to my neck. The two bottles of pills that will be my release nestle between the silver taps and I touch them with my toes, covering them in bubbles.

For a long while I lie, eyes closed in the peace and quiet, letting the heat soak through my skin, letting the water comfort me. I try to empty my thoughts, but doubt still lurks in the dark patches of my mind; I feel it probe for any weakness, trying to prevent me from doing what I'm about to do, suggesting there is a benefit to going on, but I ignore it, the strength of my convictions victorious again.

Slowly, I open my eyes and stare at the wall before me. The movement of projected flame is hypnotic, and I find myself creating pictures in the same way I used to find faces and animals in the clouds. A memory floats over me, of a summer's day, of my sister and me lying on our backs in the garden, of Ben running wild around us, and of showing her how to find stories in the sky. She used to say 'sky-sheep', because she wasn't able to say 'cloud'. I giggle at her innocence. The thought of my sister returns my mind to the moment, and I pick up the phone and dial.

She answers and immediately tells the male voice, murmuring in the background, to be quiet and to wait in the other room. She asks me how my day is (fine, thanks), how I feel (I've been better), when I'm going back to work (not sure yet), if she can get me anything (no), and do I want her to come over (not tonight, Louise). It's been the same conversation, with the same answers, twice a day for the last few days. She knows it too, and she quiets down, waiting for me to speak.

"I wanted to tell you something," I say. "I need you to let go of what happened four years ago. Okay?" Silence. "Even if we'd known what was going on in my body, would you have done anything different? Would my advice have changed? No, I honestly don't think so. You made the right choice, for the right reasons. You did the only thing you could do, Louise. You did the only thing you could."

"What's going on?" she asks. The concern in her voice is unmistakable. There is a long, long quiet between us before I answer.

"Louise, I don't hold what you did against you. I never have and I never will; even with what I know now. I have to make peace with what the doctor said, and I can't do that if I know you're regretting something from when you were sixteen that was blatantly the correct thing to do, considering the circumstances."

"Are you sure you're okay?" She speaks softly, like she's a little girl again, sneaking into my room after our mum has shouted at me for no reason.

"I'll be better once you answer my question."

She sighs, a breath of air in my ear. "There's not a day that passes when I don't wonder if I did the right thing; not a day when I don't dream how my life would be different. Think how grown-up I'd have to be! I would be a mum! Can you imagine? No more late night parties, no more forgotten weekends, no more waking up next to random guys. There's no way, even with all the support in the world, that I'd have been capable then – even now – of coping with a baby. I know

I did the right thing, sis. I know I did. Even with the news you've been given, I know I did what I had to do."

"Thank you, Louise," I croak. It's all I wanted her to say. "I love you, yeah?"

"I love you too. I hope you're okay. Call me tomorrow."

Carefully, I wrap the handset into the towel and take a deep, deep breath. My hands press gently on my empty belly, both lost under the bubbles. What I would give to know what it was like to have my child grow inside me, even for just a few hours. I wish the next few minutes away, and wipe at fresh tears.

It's time.

The two bottles of thirty sleeping pills slide down my throat three at once.

Lying back, head resting on the air-filled cushion, body covered in bubbles, my wet fingers lift the stone that has hung above my breasts since he gave me it all those years ago, a symbol of our secret engagement, the single remaining physical memory of our love. I kiss it, whispering over and over how much I love him, how much I miss him, how sorry I am we couldn't last forever.

I close my eyes. Already, things feel different, spongy, like I'm dissolving into the water. His face fills the space in my mind, I'm smothered in his smile, the scent of him washes over me in wave after wave.

Robert: My true love. You will be all I see when the light fades.

~

"You can't go yet."

The voice, familiar, echoing, pulls me back from the darkness I was falling towards.

"You know you can't go yet."

Something pushes on my eyelids, weighing them down. I

fight, I force with all my might to open them, to see the face of the voice. A thought, a realisation: The front door is locked; so is the bathroom. No one should be in here; no one.

"You can't go until you tell him goodbye."

With all the strength I have left, I barely manage to open one eye. There is a woman, naked, smiling, sitting on the edge of the bath, running her fingers through the bubbles. Something shimmers and glitters on her chest, just below her neck. I recognise it. It's mine. How did she get it? How did she manage…?

~

Blinding white light assaults the endless pitch black in which I had been hiding.

"She's responsive!"

"Get her out of there!"

Two voices, one male, the other female. Arms lift me out the still-warm water, which pours onto the tiled floor. I hear a mumble, and I realise it comes from my mouth.

"Try not to speak, okay? My name is Emily. I'm a paramedic. You called us to say you had taken an overdose. Are these the tablets you swallowed? Just nod if they are." My head feels as though it's filled with oil as I do so. "And did you take them all?" Again, I nod. "Thank you. You'll be just fine, okay? You did the right thing by phoning us and leaving the doors unlocked. You did the right thing. We're going to take you to the hospital now."

In the pale half-light of the hallway, an opaque shadow hangs over me, barely visible through the tiniest of slits in my eye-lids.

It whispers in my own voice, and as I slip into darkness once more, I understand.

"You can't let go until you tell him goodbye."

19

Hospital protocol dictated her partner wait outside whilst the doctor spoke to her. Under normal circumstances she would have wanted him to remain by her side, to hold her hand and smile as he told her everything would be fine; but she knew the circumstances were not normal. The news the doctor would explain was not something she wanted him to hear – not yet anyway. She would tell him in her own way, in her own time.

The young doctor stood next to her patient, leaning over her so that the other did not have to strain to see. There was a long silence between them: a pause, a hesitancy that could not be measured. Outside, a cloud passed over the low sun, dulling the room. The net curtain waved gently in the draft of vented air; green light blinked silently from the screen beside her. The smell of disinfectant was lessened by the fresh scent of the doctor's perfume. She wiggled her toes, felt them move beneath the sheets. It made her smile.

"I'm not going to ask you how you're feeling", the doctor began. "Something tells me you might have felt better." They smiled at each other, but the doctor hushed her when she tried to speak. "You will need your every word for the young man outside. He'll need to know most, if not all, of what I tell you; what I think you might already know."

The other nodded gently, a barely perceptible movement of her bandaged head.

"I'll begin by telling you what we did when you were brought in here. Then I'll ask you a few questions. I just need to you nod yes or no – there's no need to speak. But before I do, I want you to answer me this." The doctor made sure eye-contact was met and held before she continued. "Are you aware of anything, any medical condition you may have just now? It's important – vitally important – you tell me what you know."

There was an understanding passed between them at that moment in the deepening silence of the single room of the high-dependency unit, an understanding that required no words to be spoken other than to clarify what the other knew. There would be no secrets now, no hidden surprises; what was said now would leave nothing to remain for later.

And so she spoke, quietly, careful to tell the doctor everything she knew. As she spoke, she thought of the card left behind at the accident, of the truth it contained; and she wondered again how she would ever get the courage to say to her lover what she so easily said to this stranger now.

Chapter Nineteen

I'm eighteen. Robert has been missing from my life for over a year, and the void he left remains cold and empty. Everywhere I go I see him; he is the guy in front of me in the line at the store; he is the passenger in the car stopped at the lights. I smell his aftershave in the air, even when there is no one about. I hear his voice say my name; I hear it rise above crowds of people, only to fade unanswered into the faceless and the nameless. I taste him in drops of rain and on feather-light breezes. And at night, alone, I feel his touch; his lips on my neck and his fingers in my hair; his skin press against mine.

I wish the pain would stop.

~

I'm twenty-one. His memory still haunts me, refusing to leave, even in the wake of one-time-only dates and two-week-long relationships. With every sunset, I whisper goodnight to him, wherever he is, and hope that in the morning, somehow, a little bit of my feelings will be magically shaved off. But with each dawn, I open my eyes to the image of his face, floating before me in the dark, in the light, in the dust-filled streams of honey that slide through gaps in my blinds.

~

I'm twenty-six. Its winter; cold and dry; cloudless skies bathed in cornflower-blue; breaths visible; cheeks painted pink on pale skin; gloved hands and thick jackets; empty trees sleeping, waiting for spring. I place the magazine back in the rack and pick up its neighbour, unable to choose, unsure if any of the dozen or so before me are really that different. I thumb through the pages, absently trawling for anything of interest, when I hear my name. It's his voice, and it sings to me at the same time the cash-register rings. I smile. I'm used to it by now. There's a story on page thirty-four that catches my eye and I begin to read the first few lines. I hear my name again; his voice; louder this time; closer. A hand taps my shoulder; my name; his voice. The magazine closes in my hands. I turn round.

It's Robert. He's here.

He grins at me, looking exactly as he did on the night we last spoke. His eyes still sparkle and his smile still melts my heart. None of the youthfulness has gone from his face. He's wearing the shirt I bought him for his birthday, tucked into his jeans, hopelessly out of fashion, just as he was nine years ago. Even his trainers haven't changed.

My Robert is here.

I try to speak, but the words stick in my throat. I feel the force of everything unsaid well-up inside me, filling me to bursting point. Without losing his smile, without moving his lips, he says my name. I tilt my head slightly: Something isn't right. He hasn't moved since I turned around.

My hand reaches out to him, to touch his face. But it paws at nothing but air, passing through his image as it ripples like water.

"Robert?"

The word escapes from my lips before I can stop it, and it shatters him into a thousand shards of glass, exploding towards me. I shield my face with my arms and scream.

When I waken up, I am alone. Sweat soaks my nightshirt and damp sheets cling to me like glue. Tears stream down my cheeks as the dream, as the nightmare, dissolves into nothing.

I head into the kitchen, the heat from the radiators keeping the cold winter outside, and switch the kettle on.

Outside, the frost-covered pavements have a dull orange hue under streetlights and everything is still. The world is dreaming, fast asleep. And somewhere, I know, my Robert is too.

~

I'm twenty-nine. The events of the last twelve months still cloud my thoughts; still loom over me like an executioner's shadow. They say things get easier in time, that the pain lessens – but that's not the case at all. What happens is you become increasingly numb as, day after day, another little piece of them fades to memory, becoming less and less real. Soon, it's the guilt of not thinking about them that makes you think about them, and the hurt starts all over again.

Today, like every other day, I spend my morning in a cafe, doing my best to forget, watching the world slip by through tinted glass. The staff know me by now, and whenever I cause the little bell above the door to jingle, they start making my single-shot vanilla latte. I don't even have to speak to anyone any more, other than to say thank you when they hand me my change.

I sip the coffee and unfold a newspaper someone has left on the table beside mine. The lead story is of a house-fire in which a family of four died. There's a photograph of the grandparents laying flowers at the scene, despair chiselled onto their faces, the will to live ripped from their hearts. The lack of understanding they feel now will never leave them. Reports will be written, professional opinions published, and maybe the finger of blame will be pointed at someone or something. Lessons will be learned, they will be told; this tragedy will never occur again. But nothing will help. No words or actions can deaden the sense of loss, the sense of waste. Life, in its new guise, will be unwanted and unwelcome. The past, no matter what they do to ignore it, will be there waiting for them every time they open their eyes.

And it's a feeling I know all too well.

I scan the first few lines of the story before closing the paper and setting it to one side. My heart sinks deeper into my chest; my eyelids slide closed; my breathing fades to almost nothing. The man who lost his life, the father who died trying to save his babies, was called Robert.

I know it's not my Robert who died – both the age and surname are wrong – but I have lost almost everything this last year. The thought of losing the only thing that keeps me going wells within me. I squeeze my hands into fists as they begin to tremble. I feel sick.

And at that moment, with the light in his eyes burning away the hesitation that has kept me down for so long, with the fear of never seeing him again washing over me like an ocean's wave, I know what I must do.

Steam still spirals from my coffee and the pastry sits on the plate untouched as the bell jingles behind me for the last time and I begin the search for the man I have loved forever.

~

Mid-summer has slipped by unnoticed and the slow slide into dark nights and warm jackets has begun. This morning, in the shower, I realised the date and a nostalgic sadness swept over me. Thirteen years ago today, I was proposed to for the first and only time in my life. It seems strange, now, that I've never given the actual day a special place in my thoughts, just the event. I always remember the anniversary of our first kiss; I still smile when the date comes round of the night that never was; I can't escape the memory of when I ran from his arms for the last time. And so, with the prospect of finding my Robert becoming less and less likely, I decide to relive one of the moments in my life that defines who I am.

The drive down to the coast gives me more time to think, more time to accept there is almost nothing more I can do to locate him. Thirteen years is a long time in which to lose yourself. Old friends have been contacted, but no one has heard from him since he moved away. The university he attended could only tell me he graduated, but nothing more. And the company his father worked for went out of business years ago. I'm walking blind-folded in a labyrinth of dead-ends. I remind myself he could have found me at any time, and he hasn't. Maybe things are this way for a reason; maybe things are this way for the best.

By the time I park my car, I finally admit I may never see him again.

The pebbled shore crunches beneath my boots, the wind churns the sea, whipping salty-spray onto my face and dark, heavy thunderheads crawl low towards me. I zip my jacket against the elements and cover my head with its hood.

Recollections of thirteen years ago flood through me, provoking a smile. It still smells the same as it did then, perhaps as it has always done. I pick up a stone and throw it hard into the water, watching it vanish into the curve of a wave, sinking. For a few minutes that is all I do and I'm lost in the moment, lost like the stones that lie invisible beneath the tide. Every throw and every splash, feels therapeutic, like I'm hurling the hurt and pain of the last eighteen months into an abyss.

Before I know it I'm laughing, picking up and launching rock after rock through the air. It feels wonderful and for the first time in a long time my mind is clear, existing only in the here and now, at the beach, throwing stones into the water, taking the same joy from doing so as a child would.

A low, guttural rumble sounds from the clouds over the choppy sea and a grey blanket of rain inches closer, hiding the distant islands in a fine mist. Still grinning, I turn away from it and run in the direction of the cove Robert and I promised our lives to one another in all those years ago. I hope, as the rain darkens the gravel path around me, the little shelter, with the bench and the roof is still there.

It is, and I sprint for it, racing the weather, intentionally splashing in each and every puddle on my path. My hood flaps behind me, and by the time I reach the shelter, my jeans are soaked through and my hair is a tangled mess, matted to my face with saltwater and warm rain. I sit on the bench, catching my breath, listening to the constant drum of the rain on the roof. The huge smile remains fastened to my lips, unwilling to leave. This, I decide, is the day I finally put the past behind me.

I check my watch, waiting for the second hand to tick round four more times. And when it does, I lift my necklace out from under my jacket and kiss the stone. "Yes, Robert. One day I will marry you."

The minutes pass into an hour, the first of my new life, and as I'm about to leave, I look around the shelter, reading the various messages and scrawls of graffiti left by countless, anonymous souls over the years. As I'm scanning the names, a shadow passes behind me and stops. The hairs on the back of my neck prickle. Someone is there, waiting, unmoving at my back. My fingers search my pockets for a weapon, for any means of defending myself. I close my eyes and swallow hard against my dry mouth. How typical would it be for something to happen to me now, after taking the first steps in making peace with my life, after promising to move on from the past?

"I'm sorry I'm late."

The voice is soft. The voice is friendly.

"Every year I come here, and every year the weather is the same."

The voice is oddly familiar.

I turn around slowly. Against the bruised-yellow clouds of a July thunderstorm, with driving rain around him and an infant gale howling between us, Robert stands before me.

And this time, as my fingers touch his wet cheeks, I know for sure he is real.

20

She wanted to think of him, to spend the next few minutes thinking of nothing more than him. She wanted the gently-spoken ferocity of the doctor's words to remain in limbo as she lay still in the heavy silence of her room. She wanted to imagine their life together, to dream of a future lifted from the pages of a child's fairy tale, where they'd ride into the sunset together, spending the rest of their lives in perfect bliss.

But she couldn't do any of that. The doctor's words still rang in her ears, razor-sharp, slicing away any fibre of hope she may have harboured. There would be for her, she knew, no fairy tale ending.

The physical pain she felt was numbed by the sudden emotional stress. A morphine drip bled into the back of her hand, but nothing could lessen her sense of loss. The net curtain still waved to her left, the green light pulsed like clockwork from the monitor and the smell of bleach clung to her nostrils with an iron grip. She tilted her head slightly. There were tiny spatters of rain on the glass she could see beyond the curtain. For the first time since she was here, she wondered what day it was. She didn't know how long she had been unconscious, but suddenly, it seemed relevant. Outside, beyond the window, life continued. All the things that had mattered so much to her then, on the outside, were now insignificant: details lost in the confusion. She smacked her lips together, tasted cotton wool.

"Life," she whispered. She smiled sadly, her eyes staring at a point far beyond the ceiling. "Wherever has it gone?"

Chapter Twenty

"You look really happy," I say, rinsing the soap from my fingers, looking at my sister in the reflection of the restroom mirror.

"I am," she grins, touching-up her mascara. "Life is being really good to me right now, you know? Everything is working out in my favour, the stars are aligned, the birds are singing..."

"And you're still talking nonsense."

"And I'm still talking nonsense."

I dry my hands on a paper-towel and search my handbag for lip-gloss. Louise is a step ahead of me and offers me hers. "I'm glad you brought Amy," I say, coating my lips in sticky shine. "She's great fun."

"She is that," she says, her big blue eyes sparkling in the tiny spotlights, "and so much more."

"Either way, it's good to finally put a face to the name. You've spoken about her for long enough." I smack my lips together hand her back the make-up. The face in the mirror returns my smile. "And you were right about her, too: She really does redefine beautiful."

"I need to tell you something," she says, turning to face me, her voice low and almost apologetic. Her lips are tight together and a tiny vertical line has appeared in the space between her eyebrows. I groan inwardly. She only ever wears that expression right before she delivers some kind of verbal lightning bolt. She clears her throat. "I've wanted to..."

The restroom door opens and two women walk in. Our eyes meet and we exchange pleasantries, commenting on how wonderful the restaurant is. As they lock their separate cubicle doors, Louise looks at me. She's smiling, shaking her head. The moment has gone.

We return to our table and take our seats, Louise next to Amy, me next to our aunt. The dessert plates have been cleared away and coffee has been ordered whilst we were away.

"Amy has just invited us to watch her in her play on Friday evening," my aunt says to me. "It's my last night here and I've said we'd go. Are you free?"

"Free?" Louise laughs. "She's always free! She is the Ice Queen, frozen and dangerous! I pity any man who crosses her path!"

She bats away the napkin my aunt throws at her.

"Thank you, Amy," I say, ignoring my sister. "I'd love to come."

A waiter arrives at our table with the coffees. I sip my cappuccino and lick the froth from my lips. It tastes bitter, and four heaped spoonfuls of sugar sink into the cup to balance the flavours.

"You should try this," Louise says and slides over her tall glass.

"I've had a latte before, thank you very much."

"Just try it."

I take a mouthful of the hot liquid and it slides down my throat easily. It tastes wonderful.

"French Vanilla," Louise says, taking the glass away from me before I can steal any more. "It saves you killing the coffee with sugar."

Out the corner of her eye, the amber light of twenty-six lit candles cause Louise to turn round, just as the staff join with us in singing Happy Birthday. Her face turns scarlet as the cake is placed on the table and the other diners applaud as she blows the candles out.

"I can't believe you guys!" she says, clearly moved and painfully embarrassed.

"It was all Amy's doing," my aunt says as she picks out the candles and sets them on a side-plate.

A fork from the table beside us falls to the carpeted floor with a dull thud. Reaching down to get it, under the table, I see Amy's hand resting on my sister's thigh and my sister's hand resting on Amy's. I pause. In that instant, the last six months make sense.

Her drinking every night has all but stopped, as has the waking up beside men whose names she can't remember. She said she had found genuine happiness in herself for the first time in her life. She said she finally knew who she was.

I sit up and pass the fork back to the couple who dropped it. Louise and Amy are laughing, staring into each other like they are the only two people left alive. A smile grows on my lips as I watch them. I've never heard laughter like it – in my imagination, it's the sound made by angels' wings. My aunt nudges me and winks: She knows too. A lump builds in my throat and my heart tingles. My little sister is in love.

~

An hour later, we are in a bar in town. A bottle of Champagne chills in an ice-bucket on the middle of the table, our four glasses are already gleaming with bubbling gold. Our aunt bought it, and she raises her glass, clearing her throat.

"I've not been entirely honest with you guys," she says, and Louise and I exchange confused glances. "I didn't come back because I had a spare week of vacation time. I came to say goodbye to this place; other than you two, there is nothing here for me besides memories, and they are with me wherever I am. You can all come to visit any time you want, but this is the last time I'll be making this trip."

Her glass remains in the air and it's Louise who touches it first, followed by Amy then me.

"And that's not all," she adds before anyone else can speak. "I wanted to tell you both something, face to face; something so amazing that I couldn't bring myself to tell either of you oceans apart." Her eyes pass from mine to my sister's and back to mine. "And Amy, I'm delighted you are here to be part of this, too." She waits, then, letting the tension build, wearing a tight half-smile on her lips.

"Oh, come on!" Louise gasps. "At least tell us if it's good news!"

"No, it's not good news," she laughs. "It's great news! As you know, Adam and I have been trying for a baby for years without any luck. About eighteen months ago, we started the process of becoming adoptive parents. And a couple of weeks ago, we were accepted."

I grip my fingers around my aunt's arm, beaming with joy. Louise claps her hands together, smiling wider than I've ever seen her before.

"But that's not all," she says. "The best bit is yet to come. The young woman whose babies we are to become parents of is expecting twins: twin girls, to be exact. And Adam and I have decided to name them after you two."

It's Louise who reacts first, running round the table to wrap her arms around her aunt. Her eyes are closed and two beads of water trickle past her nose.

"Thank you," she whispers, over and over again, holding her for a long time. "Thank you." She signals to the waiter for another bottle of Champagne. When she finally takes her seat, Amy wipes her eyes.

I hug my aunt, then. Words fail me. I'm so happy for her I

could burst. She slides her arms around my back and rocks me side to side.

"I need you to know something," she says into my ear, holding me tight. "Life is never over as long as there is tomorrow. I am testament to that. When I lost your uncle, I could have ended it all; it would have been so very easy just to close my eyes and never waken up. But even though I went through so much pain then, it was worth it now. I only remember it was sore – I don't remember the actual feeling. Does that make sense? And now, things have never been better. You've got so much left to say, so much left to give. Don't let go, okay? Don't let go."

She releases me, kisses my damp cheek and holds her glass into the centre of the table again.

"To the future," she says, her voice cracking with emotion.

"To the future," Amy and Louise both echo, leaning gently into one another as they speak.

I lift my glass and touch it to theirs. "And to the memories that make us who we are."

~

Quarter past two in the morning. Neon lights above the nightclub exit flash, reflecting inverted on slick pavements. The rain slides diagonally across a black sky, a thick, heavy rain that jabs our bare skin like icy spears. My aunt pulls us into a doorway, and we huddle together, laughing at the weather like we had escaped from an institution. None of us are dressed for this; when we met earlier on, there was not a cloud in the sky and now streams flow across blocked drains and puddles swell like ponds.

"There's no way I'm waiting on a cab in this," Louise says, staring out into the dark.

"You don't have a choice," I say. My speech is slurred with

Champagne and wine. "You've had too much to drink to drive home. Besides, the four of us are soaked through already; what difference will ten minutes in a line make?"

Her eyes don't move from the sky. "I stopped drinking three hours ago. I only had water in the club."

"She's right," my aunt says, and Amy nods, too. "Every time I was at the bar, Louise ordered a bottle of still water."

"Even so," I add, "you have way too much alcohol in your system to be driving anywhere."

My sister says nothing. She chews her bottom lip, turning something over in her mind. Amy has her hand resting on the small of her back. My aunt slicks back her hair and shivers as the rain dribbles down her spine.

"Is it really worth getting pulled over and losing your licence?" I ask.

Louise looks at me, her gentle smile and big blue eyes dissolving my objection instantly. Sometimes, it's impossible to argue with her. "If there was any doubt in my mind, I wouldn't do it. Seriously, I'm fine." She unscrews the cap of the plastic water-bottle she took from the club and takes a long sip.

A memory surfaces from long ago, from when she was thirteen and our mum found her drunk in her room. No one could find the alcohol, until I drank from the bottle of water on her bedside cabinet and spat it straight back out again as the vodka burned my throat.

I'm about to ask her for a drink, just to check, when a car's horn interrupts my thoughts. It's my neighbour and her husband. She's driving, having come to pick him up after a night out and she offers me a lift back to my apartment. Louise, Amy and my aunt live in the opposite direction and they tell me to take the ride home. The rain still pummels the ground, and I'm not getting any warmer standing where I am. Reluctantly, I kiss everyone goodnight, congratulating my aunt once again and climb into the back seat of the waiting car. I wave at the three watery shadows as we drive away.

~

The buzzer rips me away from a dreamless sleep, slicing through the dark like a razor. My eyelids creak open and its a few seconds before they are able to focus on the green lights of the alarm clock. I force my tongue from the roof of my bone-dry mouth. Five fifty-seven. I wrap my robe around my shoulders and shuffle barefoot to the door, opening it before the buzzer sounds again.

And when I see the pained look in the female police officer's eyes, I crumple to the floor as my world spins violently into black.

21

Outside the room, under the fluorescent glow of pale-yellow strip-lights, he waited. At first he sat, leg twitching nervously, finger-tips drumming on the arm-rest of the plastic chair. Then he was up, pacing the short length of the waiting room, until he tired of that and absently read the various posters, leaflets and notices on the walls. He listened to the nurses' chatter, some of it professional, some of it personal and he smiled cheerfully whenever any of them passed. But his mind was set on what was happening inside her room, on the conversation between his love and her doctor.

He was still wondering, still imagining, still torturing himself with every scenario, when the door opened and the doctor stepped out.

She managed a warm but professional smile as she closed the door behind her and motioned for him to sit down. He stared at her for a second or two, confused as to why he was not allowed inside. "Just give her a minute," she said, and gestured once more to the waiting area.

She sat beside him, hands clasped on her lap. "I'll be back around in an hour or so to see how she is," she began, "but I'll need you to be strong for her. Her body has been severely traumatised and there was some excessive bleeding during the operation when she was admitted."

"Be strong for her?" he asked, and he looked genuinely puzzled. "Are you going to tell me what's going on? And of course I'll be strong for her; why would I be anything else?"

She held her hands up, placating, and nodded. "I wanted to speak with you, alone, simply to make you aware that we encountered some complications during the surgery. I can't go into details, so please don't ask, but you should know that things were not as straight-forward as anyone expected them to be."

He started to speak, and then stopped himself. There was, he realised, no point in arguing with the doctor; she had told him what she could, and getting frustrated with her would help no one. He bit his bottom lip and leaned forward in his chair.

"As I said, I'll be back round again soon to see how she – to see how you both are doing." Her voice was smooth and soft, her words pitched perfectly. It reminded him of the way his mother spoke to him when she told him his gran had died. He was only six years old, but that she was delivering bad news to him was lost in her tone. He breathed out slowly, exhaling the memory and its implications for here and now. He swallowed back the gathering tears. She rose and he stood with her. "Let the nurses know if you need anything."

He watched her go, the clip of her heels on the tiled floor fading with her. The posters on the wall were blurred, the leaflets on the little table to his left were merged into one mass and he rubbed at his eyes. He had to compose himself. He had to, in the doctor's words, be strong. The door to her room was just twelve feet away, and he took a deep breath before he made his way across the corridor. Pausing outside the door, he slid his hand into the inside pocket of his jacket. He removed the card, still in its envelope, and thumbed the edges. He should show it to her. He should let her know he had it. It was for him, after all; she had written it herself, his name neatly scribed on the pale mauve paper in her distinctive swirl. He smiled a rueful smile, placed the card back into his pocket and breathed in the sterile air.

No, he thought. There were more important things to think about now. He would show it to her in good time.

Chapter Twenty-One

I am unable to sleep – again.

My bedroom ceiling has become a blank canvas onto which I reluctantly paint the images of my past, and the dreams of my future. For hours at a time I lay, relaxed body, hyperactive mind. Aromatherapy candles and oils haven't lulled me away, strenuous workouts in the gym have failed, and puzzle books, reading, and watching television have all had little effect on my insomnia. And a massive collection of various prescription sleeping pills sit unopened and unused in my bathroom cabinet; but I physically cannot take tablets any more, not since I tried to take my own life. I have been alive for nine thousand, three hundred and forty-one days. And right now I could recall every single one of them.

With a sigh, I throw my blanket to one side and walk to the window. Opening it wide, I lean out into the night. The first scents of summer linger in the air. A full moon hides behind the iron-grey puffs of a cloud, silver scattered like glitter across its edges. Silence nestles in empty silhouettes. Not even a lonely breath of wind walks the streets tonight. Across the road, dark windows stare back at me, reflecting my mood. I wonder, briefly, what secrets shelter within.

I know I'm not going to fall asleep any time soon; the wheels of my brain still spin out of control, dragging my reluctant, tired body along in its tracks. I need to do something to pass the next few hours, something that will keep my mind busy, and something that will tire me out. I look behind me, to the car key on the dresser, and smile. After stepping into jeans and slipping on a vest-top, I tiptoe down the stairs, start the ignition and try to catch the horizon.

I avoid the artificial amber of the main roads, driving instead across the hills. Here, the night is endless black, perfect for my frame of mind. I take my time, keeping my speed low and the gear high. Rounding a corner, I suddenly have to swerve to avoid something lying on the road. If I were going any faster, I would've hit it and ended up, at best, damaging only the car. I pull over and fetch a blanket from the boot, to move whatever it is onto the verge and out of harms' way. As I walk towards it, a moon of bruised ivory creeps out from behind a cloud and bathes the scene in milky light.

A baby fox lays still, body broken, eyes closed, tongue lolling from its mouth. A pool of blood surrounds it like a moat of spilled ink. The cub is tiny; it can only be a two or three months old. I start towards it, but freeze when two bright eyes glint from the hedgerow. Another fox, the same size at the one on the road, pops its head out into the night. It tastes the air, waits, and then pads over to its sibling. A tail, almost as long as its body swishes behind it. It's beautiful, like a newborn puppy. It stares at the body on the road and at the blood that still oozes from it. It tries to bark, but a high-pitched squeak is all that emerges. I decide she's a girl. And then she sees me.

For a moment, for a long, long moment, our eyes connect and we are the only two things alive on the entire planet. We wait, unmoving until the fear of danger passes and she feels safe. She looks back to her fallen sister. With her nose, she nudges her, once, twice, and then rests her little ginger paw on her lifeless cheek. She looks up at me again. In her sad eyes, she knows the truth of the situation but knows, too, she will never understand it.

The moon slides behind a patch of cloud and life fades to grey. Her silhouette nuzzles its sister for the last time and turns, vanishing into the shadowed hedge and to the empty field beyond.

~

Miss David tells us to open our desks and take out a fresh, clean sheet of paper and our colouring crayons. As we do so, she writes something on the board and the murmur of her class of five year-olds trying to read her words rumbles like distant thunder until she asks for quiet.

She points to the letters, sounding each one as her chalk touches it.

"Class project," she says and turns to look at us. "Who can tell me what a project is?"

My arm is the only one raised and I answer. Smiling, she sticks another gold circle next to my name on the chart at the door; two more and I'll get to choose a present from the box on her desk. I get a thumbs-up from Joanne.

"And for this project, I need you all to put your thinking caps on."

We each pull imaginary caps over our ears. It's her way of getting us to concentrate, and it works like a charm. Silence waits for her to speak.

"You're each going to draw a picture for me and write a little story about it. And it's not just anything I want you to draw; I want you to draw a picture of what you want to be when you grow up. The story you write will be of why you want to be whatever it is you draw. Does everyone understand?"

The noise in the classroom swells until she puts a single finger to her lips.

"Hands up if you know what it is you're going to draw."

Twenty-five tiny arms shoot into the air. Joanne's leg bounces excitedly, shaking our desks. Miss David signals for us to lower our arms. She walks to the oversized clock on the wall and points to the twelve and the three. We have until the bell rings to do what we can, and she says if we behave tomorrow and for the rest of the week we will be allowed to spend each afternoon on it.

Immediately, I pick up my black crayon and begin to draw.

By Friday afternoon, the pictures are drawn and coloured and the two- or three-sentence stories are written. Miss David asks us, one at a time, to come to the front of the class and tell the others our dreams and aspirations of a future so distant it seems forever away.

Joanne is first to go, and she holds her drawing above her head.

"This is me," she says, looking up at the back of the paper, "on a horsey, and here's my castle and I'm a princess and I'm holding hands with a handsome prince and we are married and we live happily ever after."

She beams as the class applauds and Miss David pins her project to the wall. I believe, just as she does, that she will be a princess one day; after all, why wouldn't she be?

One by one, the class stand up to explain their ambition. And when they sit down again, their drawing on the wall, they each dream for a moment of what it will be like when they have become the nurse or the singer, the superhero or the sports star in the picture.

Everyone else has had their turn and Miss David looks at me expectantly. With a deep breath I slide my chair out from under me and walk to the board.

"This is me with a baby in my tummy and this is the house where I live and this is the sun and this is my dog and this is the pram I will push my baby around in when it's born."

"That's a lovely drawing," Miss David says, and her voice is soft and kind. "It's very bright and colourful, and I like the way you've got lots and lots of detail. But you were meant to draw what you want to be when you are older. Do you know what you want to be when you grow up?"

I look at her, embarrassed. I thought it was obvious, but maybe it's not; maybe my picture won't be stuck on the wall with the others.

"Miss David," I whisper, as though what I'm about to say might be against the rules. "I just want to be a mum."

~

Our class field-trip is finally over and we file into the gift shop. Sixteen of us in a tight, cramped space no bigger than my bedroom make the old ladies behind the counter nervous. They eye us suspiciously, especially the boys, but there's no need; our bags are outside and even if we were the kind of kids who would steal, I doubt we would; there's nothing here worth getting caught for.

I pick up a handful of dinosaur-shaped chocolate bars for my family, a packet of hard sweets for myself and a t-shirt for Louise. It has become a custom over the years, that whenever I go on a trip she expects me to bring her one back – my dad even gives me the money for them. As I pay, the lady who serves me doesn't even look at me; she's watching two boys play-fight with a couple of plastic animals. I think about saying something to her about her blatant rudeness as she drops the change into my waiting palm, but instead, I just shake my head at her and walk away. She remains oblivious.

Eventually, with our presents purchased and what little light there is quickly fading from the western sky, we climb back onto the minibus and begin the three-hour drive home.

About an hour into the journey, I open my sweets and pass

them round my friends and teachers. I'm still ranting on about how unfair it is that, just because we're young, just because we're in our early teens, we are all branded as troublemakers, thieves and delinquents. I tell Mr Bell, who is sat in front of me, he should contact the management of the museum and request an apology; he, in turn, suggests it would be more powerful and have more meaning if it came from me. So with an angry determination, I pull a notepad from my bag and begin writing. I pop two more blackcurrant sweets into my mouth, sucking hard on them for inspiration.

And then one slides down the back of my throat, lodging itself in my windpipe.

I try to breathe or to cough, but I simply cannot do either. I try harder, but there is nothing. This, I realise, must be what it feels like to choke. Fear grips me. Is this how I'm going to die?

I tap Mr Bell on the shoulder and he turns in his seat. It takes a second or two before he realises what's wrong. In one fluid movement, he is behind me and lands his clenched fist on my spine – twice – with more force than I'd ever felt before; the second time does the trick and the purple sweet falls from my mouth onto the floor. Now I can breathe, now I can cough, and for the next few minutes, I do nothing else but.

My aunt is waiting with the other parents and relatives when the bus finally pulls into the school.

I tell her about my 'near-death' experience; about the spots that appeared at the edges of my vision; about the fact Mr Bell said my lips were turning blue. And she laughs.

"Did you really think you were going to die?" she says, smirking.

I nod.

"Well, from what you've told me, I can safely say you were not in any danger of dying tonight." She laughs again at the confusion on my face. "Now, this is just my opinion, but your mind is filled with millions upon millions of memories – more, I suppose, than you could ever remember – and I believe when you're actually on your way out, you see the parts of your life that make up who you have become: Dreams; people; places; happy times; sad times – all of them memories that combine to paint the picture of the person you are."

"But I didn't have any of that tonight."

"Exactly," she says. "That's how I know you weren't going to die. And that's just as well, cos I'd miss you!"

We laugh together, and as I stare out the window at the passing blur of lights and strangers, I wonder what I will remember when it's time for my life to flash before my eyes.

22

She barely managed to smile for him when he finally went back into the room. The faintest traces of pink that had returned to her cheeks had disappeared during the conversation with the doctor. He was instantly at her side, gently kissing her forehead and holding her hand, careful of the tube that fed fluid into her body. He tried to smile for them both. A long silence sat between them, like when he first came into her room, but this time it was awkward; neither seemed to know what to say, or if they did, how to say it. But all the while, he looked at her like she was the most beautiful creature on the planet.

It was she who broke the silence first.

"I love you," she said, her voice like sandpaper rubbing against knotted wood. She winced and he squeezed her hand a little bit tighter. She forced a smile, but it looked more sad than happy.

"I know," he said. "And I know you know I love you, so I don't need to say it, do I?" She nodded, and he took a deep breath. It was their routine, and she felt glad of the familiarity. "Then I suppose I love you back."

A car horn sounded from outside the rain-spattered window, and it reminded the pair that life was marching on, in spite of their situation.

"Do you want to talk about what the doctor said?" she asked. He nodded, but his eyes said otherwise.

"Only if you want to", was his reply, and his fingers moved to the inside pocket of his jacket. Maybe now, he thought, would be a good time to ask her about the card.

"I'm not sure how or where to start," she said. His hand slid out empty from inside his jacket.

"Well," he whispered, inching closer to her. "There's no hurry. I'm going to try my best to cheer you up, and then maybe, if you're able to, you can tell me a little bit of what you remember brought you here."

Chapter Twenty-Two

It's been ten days since the accident, and still my head feels spongy, like I've borrowed it from a stranger. Nothing makes sense; nothing seems real. A thick, black fog surrounds me: a heavy mist formed by the words 'if' and 'only', and it will not recede, even for a second. I am swimming through despair, and despair right now is like setting concrete.

I push the soup that was to be my lunch across the table, far enough away that my fingertips can push it no further. It's gone cold, now; a yellow skin has formed on the surface. I stare at the bowl, at the spoon, at the slice of buttered bread and wonder, belatedly, how it might have tasted. Tears threaten once more, simply because I can't remember how long it has been sitting there.

And leaning back on the sofa, with my chin resting against my chest, I close my eyes against the dull, unending ache in my soul.

~

The first funeral was five days ago.

I sit, anonymous, in the back of the crematorium as Amy's father says goodbye to his only daughter. Twice he breaks down during his speech. Twice, he leans his forehead against the rosewood coffin and sobs. And twice, he continues on, choking back his emotions with a determination I've never seen in anyone before. Throughout, he speaks to her, not us; his hands stroking the smooth, polished wood inches above her head. Occasionally, he glances down at the front row, to his wife and to Amy's twin brother and does his best to smile. He says it is almost unthinkable to go on without her, but as a family they have to try. He says they will never come to terms with a world without her in it. He says he hopes with all his heart she is in a happier place, waiting for them. I hope she is too.

When the last words have been spoken, and the last of the tributes paid, the service concludes with her coffin sliding slowly under a red velvet curtain and into the darkness beyond; the cries of two hundred mourners, weeping like injured children, echo through the hall. That's it. It's over. She's gone.

As we file out, a framed photograph of her sits next to a small, hardback book and we each scribble a sentence or two on the blank pages. With her warm, hazel eyes drawing me in and her sweet, perfect smile melting me to my core, I write, through a wash of tears, "She loved you. We all did. It was impossible not to."

~

Three days ago, although it seems much longer now, I stood next to Adam as his wife's casket was fed into the belly of the waiting aeroplane.

His arm is wrapped around my shoulders and I lean on him, knowing if he lets go I will crumble to the cold tiled floor like a ragdoll. I feel the eyes of passers-by staring at me in confusion, then pity, as they follow our gaze out to the tarmac. I hear their comments but the words don't register. I am at the stage beyond hollow, beyond numb.

He apologises once again for taking her home now. He

apologises for not being able to be with me at the other funeral. "It will be too hard," he says. "I don't know what I'd do. I may not be able to hold my tongue." He can't understand why anyone would drive home drunk, especially in the rain, especially at night. I agree with him completely, but I have to go – I need to be there when the coffin is covered in dirt.

There will be a service for my aunt in a couple of weeks' time, where her ashes will be scattered on the site of their wedding. I'm invited, of course, and he will pay for my flights. I tell him I'll do my best to be there. He knows, as do I, that I won't be.

He hugs me, long and hard, swallowing his emotions before he walks down the gangway. I apologise, as does he, but neither of us really know why.

The plane taxis to the runway, a silver arrow under a copper sun. My aunt, the woman who shared with me so much, who showed me there was more to living than just waking up tomorrow, is leaving for the last time. Already, I miss her more than I thought possible. I remember her face, beautiful, unchanging throughout the years. I think back on her stories, on her advice, and wonder at the impact one life can have on another. And I wonder, as her life slipped away from her, what her memories were made of: the ones that told her life's story; I wonder if I was a part of them?

My hand rests on the glass. I wish, even now, I could say goodbye to her, but the word remains unsaid at the back of my throat. And then, with a silent surge of power, the wheels leave the ground and she lifts into the sky, fading into a thousand blue, gone from me forever.

~

The last of the three ceremonies took place only yesterday, and I stood at the graveside, a stranger in the storm.

All around me, dark-clothed mourners huddle under dark umbrellas; a collection of dark moods bunched beneath a darker sky. Water soaks my face, but it is not tears that bathe my cheeks – it's cold, fat drops of rain. I'm too angry to cry, even if I wanted to. I steal glances at the faces there, searching for Amy's relatives, but they have clearly decided not to come.

As the priest nears the end of his ritualistic sermon, I glance at the bowed heads around me. Everyone knows what should be said, but no one is saying it. If Adam were here, he'd speak up; he would use the words "loss" and "untimely" and "unfair" in a more honest, more realistic and truthful way than they have been today. He would let everyone here know about the lives that were taken and the pain we feel.

The coffin is lowered slowly, gingerly, into the hole. The last of the three to die that night inches out of my sight and I feel my stomach lurch. Handfuls of earth are scattered onto it as the weeping becomes more audible and as one by one, the crowd disperses. I wait by the graveside until I am the only one left, then I step to the edge and stare down into the black. Rainwater streams down my nose in a steady line; my drenched clothes cling to me like a second skin; my body trembles with cold. A single word hangs from the tip of my tongue, waiting to be spoken, waiting to be released.

"Murderer."

It's out before I can think about it, a lonely sound drowned out by the steady drum of the storm. And at that exact moment, at the instant the word fell from my lips, I feel a hand rest gently on my shoulder.

I turn, and I'm face to face with my sister.

~

From down the hall, the toilet flushes and I am swept back to the present, the memories of the last week scattering like ashes in a gale. Louise comes into the living room and sits beside me. She stares straight ahead, still unable to speak, and rocks gently back and forth. I put my arm around her and rock with her, reminding myself I am her big sister and I need to be strong for her.

Her skin is so pale, it's almost transparent. A fresh white dressing is taped to her forehead above her swollen, purple eyes and the cut on her lip glistens with new blood from where she picked at the scab. I reach for a tissue and dab at it.

"How are you feeling today?" My words sound flat. She says nothing.

Twenty-four hours ago, she checked herself out of the hospital against the wishes of the medical staff. She didn't speak a single word during her time there, and she hasn't spoken to me so far either. The doctors say she is suffering from post-traumatic stress, being the only survivor of the crash. They say she will return to her normal self in time, when she is ready, when the guilt she feels starts to fade. But their labelling, their reassurances, do nothing to stop me worrying about her.

"Maybe, if you're up to it, we could go for a walk this afternoon? I don't want to force you, but it's the first nice day in ages; it would be a shame to let it go to waste."

Silence is a sound unique to itself, and it spreads anew like smoke in the air around us. I wait a few minutes before I try again.

"Louise," I turn to face her and rest my hands on hers, on her lap. "I can't imagine what it's like for you – so I'm not going to try – but you lived, and life, however obscure it seems just now, must go on. You know that, don't you? You know I'm right."

Her eyes don't even flicker, remaining locked on some distant place. With a long, deep breath, I continue.

"And I know it's still a bit soon, but we need to talk about whether or not we're going to our aunt's service. Do you think you're up for it? I'll be honest with you, I'm not sure I am, but if you want to go, I'll go and we can be there for one another, okay?" I pat her hands and force a smile. "And one last thing whilst I have your undivided attention: I need you to know this is hard for me too."

Still she says nothing and does nothing, still, apart from her slight shuffle back and forth. I get up, lift the soup bowl and walk to the kitchen to make us some tea. As the kettle boils, as another single tear slips from my chin and onto the floor, she comes in and stands behind me. Her arms wrap around my waist, her head rests at the base of my neck, and she holds me tight. Her body shakes as she weeps, but I don't move. She's my little sister again, stripped bare of all the hassles and dramas that have consumed her life over the years, simply asking for my help, and I wipe at the tears that blind me.

"Save me," she whispers, in the tiny, child's voice that fills my mind with images of our aunt and our uncle and the sound of forgotten laughter. "Save me."

I spin in her arms and hug her as hard as I can.

And for a long, long time, the empty silence that found a home in mine is gone, replaced by the painful, aching sobs of two sisters, who hold on to one another for dear life.

~

My sister kills herself on a Tuesday afternoon, less than a month after Amy, our aunt and the drunk who crashed into them all died.

She waits until I am out for a few hours, ("shopping then a bite to eat with the girls from work – are you sure you don't want to come? Okay, give me a hug. I love you too.") and empties my bathroom cabinet of the two-dozen bottles of sleeping pills I've collected over the years into her bag. Then, leaving a note for me on the coffee table, she drives out into the countryside, parks the car in a secluded section of forest and swallows every single tablet with gulps of vodka.

The police find her the next day. It's the same policewoman who told me about the crash who rings my doorbell, and after emptying my stomach into the bathroom sink, I sit with her in my living room, hollow and drained and empty of life. Together, we read the note, word by word, line by line, again and again. I tell her I had a feeling she was going to do something like this. She tells me there is nothing anyone can do to stop someone who really wants to take their own life. I nod and wipe my eyes with the sleeve of my blouse.

~

Before her funeral, I visit the coffin. The sombre, black-suited members of staff stand behind me at a respectful distance, allowing me a few final moments with all that remains of my family.

I look down at her, sleeping peacefully, her brushed-pink cheeks and glossy lips suggesting life that I know is not there. A lifetime of memories glides through my mind, tumbling into one another like dominos. I hear her squeal with laughter at inappropriate moments, cry at television commercials and sing so sweetly that entire audiences hold their collective breath. I see her wave from our aunt's garden, smiling proudly with a rake in her hand, on the night our uncle died. I see an innocence reflected in her blue eyes; I see a hidden world of mischief behind them. I feel her touch, reassuring me everything will be fine; pleading with me for help when she can't find the words. And my heart tingles as I remember each of a hundred times, running up the path, excited to see her after a trip or a day out. She was always my best friend.

Soft footsteps sound behind me. A stranger's gentle voice: "It's time."

Tears gather in my throat, choking me, and spill from my eyes. Slowly, I reach into my bag and one at a time, I remove the three things she wrote in her note that she wanted to be buried with. In her left hand, I place the smooth green rock with red and gold circles that I found for her on holiday – she loved the story of how I got it, laughing despite the fact I almost died. On her chest, I lay a photo of her, our aunt, Amy and me, taken by a waiter on the night they died. And under her right arm, where she can hold onto him and he'll keep her safe forever, I slide her old, worn, stripy-pyjama Panda.

I look at my baby sister, beautiful even through a haze, and lean in to kiss her forehead. My fingers stroke her hair. I remember her as she was, is and always will be.

"You asked to be saved so many times, Louise," I whisper through a sad smile, her child-like voice running though my head. "I'm so, so sorry I failed you. But thank you for letting me try."

Then I stand back as the wooden lid is closed before me and my little sister vanishes into the ever after.

23

*S*he didn't get the chance to let him know what the doctor said.

He was telling her a story of how a guy in his work had fallen over, taking not only an entire shelf of stationery with him, but the painfully uptight accounts director too, when she realised something was wrong.

He was laughing, laughing as though they didn't have a care in the world, and she was lost in the sparkle of his green eyes, reminded once more of how much she loved him, when the numbness started. She realised it first in her hands; there was no feeling when he stroked her fingers with his own. As he spoke, unaware, she tried to wiggle her toes, but couldn't. Doing her best to smile along with him as he spoke, she tried to relax. She did her best to lift her left arm, the one furthest from him, but it was as though it was glued to her bed. Pins and needles danced the length of her spine, settling in the back of her neck. She took the deepest breath she could, but it was shallow and broken. She caught his eye then, and something passed between them. He stopped talking mid-sentence.

"I need you to know I have never loved anyone as much as I love you", she whispered. "You have been my life, even when we were apart, and I don't think I've ever said thank you for that."

Confusion lined his face in a furrowed brow and down-turned

lips. He began to speak, and then stopped. Tears sprang to his eyes. He shook his head.

"So, thank you." The words escaped from her lips as a breath of air.

He would remember the following moment as clearly as if he had lived it a hundred times, a tiny instant that seemed to last an eternity. He was aware of her, his love, lying bruised and broken on the bed, yet never looking more beautiful. He was aware of the air from the heating unit brush at the net curtain; of the raindrops that dashed the window in dark splashes; of the sudden, deep, suffocating silence that pressed down on them both. And he was aware of the look she gave him, her eyes communicating more than an encyclopaedia ever could.

Her lips tried to smile for him as she faded away. He wiped his eyes, helpless.

"My beautiful Robert; my fiancé; my reason; my life," she breathed. "I love you."

With her last ounce of strength, she squeezed his hand. In her mind, she released the arrow from the bow and watched it fly far through the air, to land under the thick branches of an ancient oak tree.

As her eyes gently closed, an alarm sounded as a deafening monotone that filled the room. He looked at her, still not truly understanding. He looked at the steady, flat, single green line on the monitor, where it was peaking regularly just seconds ago. He shook her hand, but it was limp and heavy. He stood with such force his chair fell backwards as reality dawned.

"No", he said. "No, don't you dare! You can't leave me – not now, not ever! You've not even said..."

He ran to the door, opening it as a team of medical staff, including the young doctor from before, pushed past him. Their eyes met for the briefest instant, and he knew.

Slowly, he backed into the corner of the room, the palms of his hands pressed against his temples, his eyes unable to believe what they were seeing. As his shoulders brushed the walls, he slid down to sit on the cold floor. Never in his life had he felt so helpless, so empty.

As his future lay dying less then fifteen feet away, without thinking about it, he lifted the mauve envelope from his pocket, tore open the seal and with trembling fingers, removed the card.

Chapter Twenty-Three

Each morning, when I open my eyes and remember who and where I am, I reach across to where an empty pillow lay for years and touch him. I don't do this because I need to be sure he's still there or to check that the last fifteen months have not been a dream; I do it because I know he likes me to; I do it because I am so very much in love with him. And this morning is just like all the others.

He smiles as my fingers brush the two-day-old stubble on his cheek, lifting him from sleep and he takes my hand in his and gently kisses each of my fingertips.

"I was dreaming about you," he mumbles, stifling a yawn. I know he wasn't.

"And I was dreaming about you." He knows I wasn't.

It's the only lie we tell one another, and we tell it every single day. It was his idea. He says it's human nature to lie, to create some measure of fantasy regardless of how happy you are; he thinks that if you tell one lie a day, it satisfies the need to invent, and so far, it has worked – I have never told him anything that was not the complete truth, and he has done the same with me.

I shuffle over to him and rest my head on his chest, sliding my bare leg over his. His breath feels warm on the top of my head. Within seconds, his breathing deepens, his heartbeat slows, and he drifts back to sleep.

I let my eyes close, let his warmth soak through me, and join him, sound asleep and smiling.

We get up at around ten o'clock. A bright sun beams through the windows at the front of our home, but it looks empty of any kind of heat. I pull on a woollen sweater over my top and slide into my ankle-boots. From upstairs, I hear the shower run; that gives me at least twenty minutes before he's ready to leave. So with a deep, determined breath, I continue my search.

Somewhere in this house, probably stuck behind a cushion or tangled-up in the fabric of one of my blouses, is my necklace.

I woke up two mornings ago, and my neck felt bare. Together, Robert and I checked the sheets, looked under the mattress, and combed over every inch of our clothes from the day before. I swore to him I had it on when I went to bed, but that vow was based on nothing more than the knowledge I never, ever take it off. And now, forty-eight hours on, I'm not so sure; I genuinely don't remember the last time I was consciously aware of it. The prospect of our necklace being lost forever is heart-breaking.

Robert is being great with me. Although I know he is upset, he is not showing it; instead, he constantly reassures me not to worry, that if it's gone, it's gone and there's nothing we can do about it. I wish I could think like that, but both the necklace and what it stands for have been a part of me for so long that I simply can't. And so I keep searching, keep hoping it will turn up in the hem of a nightdress or in the fold of a towel.

Soon, a clean-shaven Robert bounds down the stairs two at a time and comes up behind me. He slides his arms around my waist and kisses my neck.

"You taste different," he says, smacking his lips together. I turn to face him, thinking if I'd changed shower cream or tried out a new perfume. But then I push him away, trying not to smile with him when he says, "a lot less metallic."

Still laughing away at his own joke, he sits on the couch and ties his laces.

"Listen," he says, patting the seat beside him for me to sit down; I do so, and he kisses me on the mouth, tenderly, passionately, the way I like it, the way that still makes the bottom of my belly tingle. When he stops, I lean back and as he speaks, the feeling lingers.

"I read a story about a woman who, about fifty years ago, lost her wedding ring. She and her husband looked for it for weeks, even checking the drains outside – no, don't go getting any ideas, we're not doing that – but it remained lost to them. So they saved up and eventually bought another one. Over the years, they had a family, and their children grew and had children of their own; but the old couple remained in the same house they had lived in their whole lives. So, one day, the youngest grandchild, a girl of three or four, was playing in the flowers at the bottom of the garden, when she ran in to her grandmother, shouting 'I found treasure, I found treasure!' And when she opened her tiny hand, there, to the woman's amazement, was her old wedding ring, covered in soil, returned to her after half a century."

"You're telling me I'm not going to find my necklace until I'm in my eighties? That's not much use to me – what if I drop dead tomorrow? I want to find it now!"

He looks at me and shakes his head, a half smile across his lips. Then he gets up and holds his hand out for me. "You're not going to drop dead tomorrow – you're much too pretty. All I'm saying is that you should never give up hope on finding whatever it is you've lost. I mean, look at us; we found one another after years of wishing, didn't we?"

I nod and hug him. He lifts me up and I wrap my legs around his waist. Still holding me, he walks to the hallway. At the foot of the stairs, with the front door to our left and with a knowing glint in his eye, he puts his mouth to my ear and whispers, "up or out?"

I don't need to reply – my smirk says all I need to say – and we laugh together as he carries me up to our bedroom.

~

A couple of hours later and Robert and I are, again, ready to leave. I am pushing him out of the house, ignoring his renewed "up or out" comment, when the phone rings.

I leave him at the opened door, pick up the phone and when the caller identifies themselves as being from the hospital, I turn my back on my partner. From outside, cold air sweeps through the living room like invisible shards of ice; my free hand rubs the back of my neck. I keep my voice low.

"Yes, this is she... That's correct... Yes, I can be there tomorrow... It might be difficult then... Could we make it later, say after three...? Half past is perfect... Do I need to bring anything...? Fine... Are you able to tell me if it's good news, or...? No, I know you can't... I'm sorry, I shouldn't have asked; I'm just nervous... Okay, thanks for calling."

I place the handset back onto the charger and take a long, deep breath.

"Is everything all right?" Robert asks from the doorway. I can't be sure what he heard, if anything, but I can't tell him yet.

"Yes, everything is fine," I say, forcing a calm smile as I walk towards him and the white lie spills from my tongue. "It was the doctor's surgery. They want me to go in tomorrow to discuss some test results. It's nothing, honestly."

"Test results? You didn't tell me you were having tests." The pained look on his face and his undisguised concern is touching, and it makes me love him a little bit more – but I laugh nonetheless.

"Robert, there's no need to worry. It's, well, it's girl's stuff." I know this will stifle his hunger for more information, and it is, in a way, the truth. It works. He holds his hands up in surrender.

"As long as you know I'm here for you, whatever you need. And if you want to talk about anything, you only need to say."

"Thank you," I say, and I lean in to kiss him. "Unless I want to talk about girl's stuff."

He laughs, and his smile lights up his face like the sun. His arms hold me tight and for a second, I'm lost in his eyes. "Anything else, we can discuss, but come on, what do I know about that kind of thing?"

I flick my tongue against his, and give him my most seductive, sultry look. "You know more than enough, my boy. More than enough."

~

I do my best to put thoughts of tomorrow out of my mind and focus on Robert.

Every week we make sure we have at least one day off work together, and we devote that time to us, to each other. It doesn't have to be anything special – we don't even need to leave the house – but it makes us appreciate that we've been given a second chance at us; it reminds us that apart, we are merely half of something magical. And today, he is treating me to lunch at one of my favourite Chinese restaurants.

It's in the mall, and on the way there we stop off at a store where he spends far too much money on things for tomorrow night. I joke with him that he secretly bought most of the sweets and chocolate for himself; he smiles like a little boy, and doesn't deny it.

After lunch, with the taste of my dessert of hot fudge cake and cream still in my mouth, we wander around for a while, window shopping. He holds my hand as we walk, pointing out clothes or shoes or bags that I'd like, telling me how much they would suit me. He thinks I'm pretty. Sometimes he pulls me into him and kisses me, telling me how lucky he is to be with me and that he has never stopped loving me. He makes me feel special, like I am the most important person in the world. Being in love with him is the simplest, easiest, most natural thing I have ever done.

Soon, we pass by the jewellers where, almost fifteen years ago, we picked out the necklace that would symbolise our love – the necklace I have somehow managed to lose in the last few days.

We stand at the doorway, smoke-grey glass reflecting us as shadows.

"Do you think he still works here?" Robert asks. He lifts his eyebrows.

"Who? The old man who served us?" I laugh as I shake my head. "No way; absolutely no way. He was about three hundred years old when we were here last time. If he's still alive he's doing well, never mind holding down a job."

But before I can stop him, he's dragging me in through the door.

I gasp, wide-eyed. Nothing appears to be any different from how it was way back then. The smell is exactly the same, the displays look identical and the decor seems to be unchanged. For a second, I am sixteen again. Robert nudges me and winks when he sees the nostalgia in my smile.

"Remember?" is all he says.

We wander around, looking down at the counters, pointing at various bits and pieces, when a voice sounds from a dark doorway at the back of the store.

"Well, well, well. Look who it is!" The old man shuffles

forwards and into the light. "And how wonderful it is to see you're still together after all these years." His hands are clasped before him and his smile draws us in.

"Hello again," I say, leading Robert over to him. "I can't believe you remember us!"

"Or that I'm still here?" he chuckles; I feel my cheeks flush. "And of course I remember you – it is difficult to forget such a thing." His grey hair has turned white and is thinner now than it was; it still dances above his ears when he moves. But his eyes have not changed and they still sparkle in the sharp spotlights of his displays. "You see, I've been doing this for a long, long time, and during that time, I have met hundreds and hundreds of couples who clearly love one another; couples who, deep in their hearts, know that loving their partner is as far as their relationship can go. But every so often, rarer even than the rays of the blue moon, I find myself in the presence of the truest kind of love, the love that will last forever – I meet a couple, *in love*, just like you two were, are and always will be."

Robert squeezes my hand and kisses my cheek.

"You're good," I say to the old man, who simply bows his head. "You're really, really good."

"And right, too," Robert adds. "We may not have been together physically over the years, but in my mind, we've never ever been apart."

If anyone else was to have said those words, I'd say they were being ridiculously sentimental or overly romantic; but it's hard to think that about Robert, when I feel exactly the same.

"So what brings you both here today?" the old man asks me. "Or are we simply browsing?"

"Well..."

"Do you remember the necklace we bought?" Robert cuts in. "The one I said was for my mum, but it was really for her?"

The old man nods once and his smile grows. "Well, she's lost it." Robert spits out the sentence and I stare at him. He looks at me, eyebrows raised. "What? Well, you have, haven't you?"

I smile apologetically at the old man and elbow Robert in his ribs. "It's not lost, as such. I just don't know where it is right now."

"Well," he laughs, "why don't you have a little look around, just in case there's anything that catches your eye. I promise to do you the best deal I can, should you find something to replace it with."

Robert lets my hand go and gestures to the display units by the door. I feel railroaded into something.

"Fine," I say as I stroll to the other end of the floor. "But I know I won't find anything."

Absently, muttering how I don't even want to look at the necklaces, never mind choose a replacement, I search the cabinets. Within a few moments, Robert joins me. He's smiling, clearly proud of something I know nothing about, and he kisses my forehead.

"Goodbye, you two," the old man says, waving. "And you," he says, nodding towards me, "good luck!"

With that, I'm ushered out the store and into the bright, sunlit mall.

Every six weeks or so, we revisit the little shelter where Robert proposed to me a lifetime ago and where we met again last summer. It's not a definite, once-a-month, cancel-all-other-plans type of thing; it's just somewhere we go when the mood takes us, where we can be reminded of how lucky we are to have found one another in a world so full of people.

And today, the mood takes us.

On the journey down, we talk about how amazing it is that the old man remembers us, and Robert wears the same enigmatic, 'I know something you don't know' smile that has sat across his lips since we left the jewellers. I ask him about it, but he shrugs his shoulders and says he doesn't know why he's smiling – he just is.

As twilight slides across the crystal blue, we park the car and throw a few stones into the waves. It's cold, and our laughter floats skyward in tiny pockets of swirling mist.

"Remember the rain?" he asks, as we begin to walk the gravel path to the shelter. "And the storm?"

"I remember everything." I take a deep breath through my nose and hold it for a few seconds. I breathe out the sea air, feeling the welcome, cleansing chill in my lungs.

"Everything?"

"Everything."

He nods as though deep in thought, and kisses my cheek. "Then you'll remember how I beat you to the bench."

With that, we race. I sprint as fast as I can, but Robert seems to be at nothing more than a quick jog. He knows how bad I am at running, and so this time, like all the other times before, he lets me win.

Out of breath, my chest heaving and my heart pounding in my ears, I sit on the bench with my head on his shoulder and watch night fall. I think about speaking to him about something that's been on my mind since the phone-call I received this afternoon. He pulls me closer, and we snuggle together as one by one, stars appear on the darkening sky.

"Do you have any regrets?" I ask, suddenly, my voice a whisper that shatters the long comfortable silence between us. "I mean, you know, about not being able to have children with me?"

I feel him smile.

"Do you really need me to answer that?"

I nod. Twice.

"Then sit up for a second, please. I have something to tell you."

I do as he says and search his face before he speaks. What he is about to say to me is serious – there is no sign of an impending joke, no signal that he's about to make fun.

"No, is the short answer," he says. "I spent the whole of my twenties searching for something that would compare to how I felt about you. I had relationships, as you know, with women who already had children, and I had a wonderful time being with them, as part of their family, watching their kids grow. But I never, ever felt the urge to have a child with them. For me, there was only one person I'd want to have a family with." He strokes my cheek and places the softest kiss on my lips. I close my eyes as he continues.

"And when we found each other again, I was so involved in *you*, I was so happy, that us having children was not even a part of my thoughts. Make sense?"

I nod and hug him hard.

"I am in love with you, not because you could one day be a mother to our children, but because I can't imagine my life having any meaning without you in it. I know we would have made excellent parents, and you know I would have loved to have been a dad, but what will be, will be – isn't that what they say? Anyway, you're the one always telling me to believe in hope, aren't you?"

"Thank you," I whisper and our lips meet anew.

The sky is dark now, the light chased beyond the horizon. I think about suggesting it's time to go, when he clears his throat.

"I have to tell you something else; something I have not been totally honest with you about." His words bring me down like lead weights on a balloon. He reaches into his pocket and removes something, placing it into my hand. I open my fingers and gasp as my necklace nestles in my palm. I hold it up, surprised, shocked, but grinning.

"You found it! I can't believe you found it! Where was it?

When did you..." I stop. Something is wrong. My eyes run the length of the chain, searching; my fingers feel, too. I quickly realise the stone is missing.

"I took it off your neck while you were sleeping," he says. "I needed to borrow it for a few days. I'm sorry to have made you think you'd lost it, I truly am."

"But the stone... Why..."

He says my name three times, softly, stopping me speaking. We look at one another for the longest time. And then, slowly, without taking his eyes from mine, he drops to one knee, and removes a tiny box from his pocket. He opens it to reveal a ring – and it has the stone from my necklace set into it.

I put my hands to my cheeks.

"The old man at the jewellers made this for us; it really is a one-of-a-kind. He didn't even charge me for his time, he was just glad we were still together. I hope you forgive me for putting you through these last couple of days. So, here goes: will you agree to share however long we have left of our lives with one another? Will you let me be your husband? Will you complete my happiness and marry me?"

He slides the ring onto my finger and with happiness leaking from my eyes, I kiss him with every ounce of love I have.

And tonight, on the eve of Halloween, laughing together as we agree to not keep our engagement secret this time, I know I have lived the happiest moment of my entire life.

24

From the opposite corner of the room, she watched him slide down the wall and lift his hands to his head. She watched him as the anguish on his face spread, as the medical staff tried to revive her flesh-and-blood self. She watched his trembling hands reach into his pocket, watched as they removed the mauve envelope. She watched him for a long, long time. He didn't know she was there, of course, but she watched him nonetheless.

The team of doctors and nurses worked hard on her, the stress of their efforts telling on their expressions, their eyes mirroring the growing sadness and frustration each one felt. The young doctor who had spoken to her earlier placed two paddles on her chest and the body heaved upwards, but the monotone remained.

She watched him as he opened the card, watched as he read the six words that were meant to change his life forever, watched as he unfolded the letter and scanned that too. She watched as his eyes filled with tears, watched as he lifted his hand to cover his mouth, watched as he tried to suppress the pain.

A voice from the bedside barked an order and a nurse ran from the room, returning seconds later with a clear bag of fluid. The same voice was speaking to her, urging her to come back to them, willing her not to go. The monotone seemed louder than before, more pronounced, more severe, like a crescendo to an inevitable ending.

She wanted to reach out to him, to touch him, to feel the jagged stubble on his cheeks, to run her fingers through his hair one last time. She wanted to kiss him and tell him how much she was in love with him, and to hear him say it in return. She wanted, more than anything else, just to hold him.

All the normal noises in the hospital were dull and distant, as if somehow removed from their location and placed in a room at the end of the corridor, with the door locked shut. A voice said, "One last time," and the figures round the body stood back as it jerked violently. They waited for a long second, but the monotone that echoed the single straight line on the monitor was all that remained.

She watched as he wept and tried to imagine how he would be feeling, picturing the images that might flash through his mind: Memories of happier times and happier places; memories of stolen moments and second chances; memories that whispered promises of forever and of touches that sparked alive with electricity. She knew how much he loved her and at once she felt a sudden ache in the deepest part of her soul.

Then a memory surfaced in her, a memory sparked by the pain she felt, and the words of her mother, spoken more than twenty years previous, rang through her mind: "Never say goodbye... Be careful what you love... It will only leave you in the end." With the sense of emptiness inside her spreading, she wondered how she would feel if she were to have lost him.

And as she stared into the depths of his emerald eyes, she realised she had – and with her life-long misunderstanding of her mother's words burning bright in her, she knew what she had to do.

Chapter Twenty-Four

My cheeks sting with the cold October air, and I pass through my breath as it folds and twists before me. Although the bags aren't heavy, the handles cut into my fingers through my woollen gloves, and the constant scraping of my heels on the pavement means I'm getting tired; I find myself stopping more often than I thought I would. But I'm buoyed by what the consultant told me, I'm still on a high after last night, and so I press on regardless.

People pass me, strangers, on foot and in cars, and I wonder if they can tell how happy I am; I wonder if they know, just by looking at me, how wonderful my life has become in the last twenty-four hours.

I stop once more under the pale orange glow of a streetlight and set the bags on the ground. Shaking my hands, I let the blood return to my fingers and I arch my back to chase the tightness from my shoulders. Above me, hidden for a moment beyond the amber hue, countless stars dust the cloudless sky; by morning, everything will be white with frost, sparkling in the low, cold sun. And by morning, if everything goes to plan tonight, Robert will be the happiest man in the world.

I pull my hat down over my ears, lift the collar of my coat up, and begin walking again, faster this time, anxious to get home. Already, witches and devils, superheroes and princesses are knocking on doors and the children squeal as their little bags are filled with chocolates and treats: a reward for them dressing up. I smile and shake my head. I've never understood Halloween, the costumes and the pretence. But Robert loves it. He says it's the one night a year where everyone can be a child for the night, without fear, without embarrassment.

Robert: My thoughts stray to the card in my bag and to his reaction, to every 'what-if' and every 'could be' imaginable. He will be suspicious – I have only cooked for him once before, for his birthday – but hopefully he will think it's because of last night. I picture him, the confusion in his eyes as I slide the card across to him, the furrow on his brow as he reads my words, and his complete disbelief and surprise as he sees the truth of them echoed in my face.

I am truly excited. I have everything I ever wanted. My dreams are fulfilled, and I have never been as happy in all my life as I am right now. Two things are testament to that fact: The ring on the third finger of my left hand, and the implications of the card I've written him. Is this what it feels like to be complete? Is this what it feels like to be at peace?

Then a scream fills the air, a scream born of a terror I've never heard before. I look across the road as a boy dressed as a pirate runs towards me from between two parked cars. He glows white in the beam of an oncoming vehicle – and then he stops, petrified, staring into the light.

Another scream, this time it's tyres sliding on icy tarmac. I look across the road – everything is slow, there is no need to rush, no need to panic – and I see the boy's mother reach out to him, her feet planted firmly on the pavement, frozen with fear; her eyes like saucers and her mouth opened wide. I recognise her. It's Sophie, my consultant's daughter. It was her who screamed first.

I hear the bags hit the ground before I realise I've let them go. Was that the bottle breaking? I'm suddenly aware of everything: of my life, of my senses and of my world. The memories of all that has ever mattered to me gather, like tiny floating lights that remind me who I am, and I smile at each and every one of them. I feel my engagement ring burn in my heart. I feel the life inside hold on to me. I feel as though I am finally home.

The night my sister is born. I'm there, living it anew, tasting the tastes, smelling the smells and feeling everything as if for the first time. It brings a smile to my face.

Then I sprint out onto the road, three steps and he's in my arms. I turn my back to the light and wait.

"Save him," I whisper behind closed eyes. "Please, save him."

25

One by one the doctors and nurses stopped working on her and stood back as an anonymous finger pressed the button and silenced the monotonous drone for the last time. One by one they filed from the room, leaving him alone with her to say goodbye. One by one, they made sympathetic eye contact with him until at last, the door closed behind him.

The tubes remained in her arms. The monitor, which had blinked green for so many hours, was now a single line. The heating unit had switched off; the net curtain above it hung limp and unmoving. Outside, darkness had fallen and the rain had stopped. Everything, it seemed, had ground to a silent halt.

He looked at her. Lying there, peaceful and still, she could have been asleep. He wished and prayed she was.

In four short steps he was at her side. His hand hovered above hers, a chasm measured in inches. He held his breath and bit his bottom lip. He didn't want to touch her. By touching her, he would be admitting to himself she was gone from his life forever. A thousand memories of her burned through his mind at once, a thousand tiny voices all crying out together. There was nothing he could do to stop them; there was no way he could distinguish between them. A single wet line ran down his cheek. His jaw quivered. And then gently, ever so gently, he placed his hand in hers.

~

She watched as the medical staff slipped quietly from the room, leaving him in peace. She watched as he moved towards her, watched as he hesitated for a long moment before summoning the strength to hold her hand. His face was etched in pain. She knew exactly how he felt – although she knew his loss was greater than hers. She thought of the love she felt for him, of the love that existed between them, and suddenly it was more powerful, more intense than anything that had existed before. All over the world, people searched for what she and Robert had – most never found it, and even more didn't believe it existed – yet here she was, drowning in it. She stared at him some more, then suddenly a feeling she had never felt before washed over her, a feeling of complete and utter peace. She felt something shift and break apart inside of her, and a wave of understanding consumed her.

It was time for her to go.

With the saddest of smiles teasing the edges of her lips, she closed her eyes and moved forward.

~

Tears came freely as grief consumed him. His shoulders shook and his stomach lurched. He let out a long, low moan. He had never felt agony like this. He leaned over her, resting his forehead on hers. She was still warm and he kissed her cheek, tasting the saltwater from his eyes.

"Please," he sobbed. "Please don't leave me. You can't let us go, not after what we've found, not after this."

He lifted the card up to her face and read to her the six words that were to have changed their lives, over and over again.

"You wrote this," he said, and placed the card on her breast. "You wrote this for me, for us and for our future. You're the one who always spoke about destiny and forever. You're the one who believed!"

He felt something brush his cheek, then, something softer than the finest silk, warmer than the whisper of summers' wind and at the sensation his heart began to pound in his ears. The hairs on his arms stood on end. He stopped talking and lifted his head. The room had changed somehow: The net curtain still hung limp; empty darkness still waited without; the thick, heavy silence still remained, yet something was different.

Then he heard it. It was her voice, definitely her voice, breathing a single word in his ear over and over again.

"Goodbye," she whispered. "Goodbye."

He felt her arms wrap around his shoulders, felt the warmth of her cheek on his. He closed his eyes and soaked in her one last time.

"Goodbye," he mouthed, unable to speak.

And with that, he felt her light fade to emptiness, to leave him to go on without her, richer and happier for sharing, eternally grateful for what little time they had.

Acknowledgements

I love reading this bit of books. For me, it's like the photographs in an autobiography – I always flick to it first. Maybe it makes reading the book more personal... or maybe I'm just nosey. I don't know.

Usually, it's "thanks to my editor, publisher, etc, for believing in me..." but sometimes, you get a proper insight into the person the author is, or what their motivation was or who they were inspired by. Sometimes, this is actually better then the novel!

So when I was thinking about publishing A Thousand Blue, I decided to think about this as my "Oscar speech". I doubt I'll write another book, and with that in mind, I wanted to make these pages something to remember – something to put smiles on faces. I wrestled over the order of the names, because I don't want to offend anyone – if it makes any difference, you're all first! And I've tried by best not to miss anyone out, so I sincerely apologise if you look for your name and it's not there. The chances are it was accidental... but there is also the possibility I just don't like you!

In short, this book is a piece of me, for all of you. Thank you to everyone who read it in advance of publication and thank you to you for reading it now.

I do hope you enjoyed it!

Acknowledgements

Debbie Moir... In a parallel universe, things are different. Everything I said to you, I meant completely. You know what you mean to me. Until the next time...
Giulietta Pirolli, Rhona Dunn & Jacqui Salter ... Life would be proper rubbish without you. Thank you for everything you have done for me over the years. I'll never be able to repay it, but I won't stop trying.
Amanda Jowett... What can I say? You are such an amazing person, and I wish everyone could have a friend like you. I'm very, very lucky to know you, and you have no idea how much I miss you.
My mum, Fiona... Without your support, I would not be where I am. Words aren't enough.
Moira and Karen... You may be family, but you are first and foremost my friends. Thank you for all your help, your support, and for letting me moan on a regular basis!
Wee Al, Jennifer, Olivia, Jake & Tristyn... It makes a huge difference to me knowing that you are just a phone call away.
Big Al, Cathy, Janette & Marty... Not a day goes by that I don't think of you all. It's not enough to say thank you, but that is all I have.

Paul, Neil, Simon & Karen Fraser... My second family. I'm really sorry things didn't work out, but I had a great time knowing you all.

Ian Maxwell... The world needs more like you. You're my friend, and I will never be able to thank you enough for giving me the opportunity when you did.

Sharon Dunn... I'm glad we had one another to remind ourselves it wasn't our fault! You truly are one of the good guys.

Elinor Wilson... I hope the meaning is never, ever lost to you. You deserve the world.

Emily & Liam Moir... I love you guys. It's been brilliant to watch you both grow, and I'm proud of who you are.

Carlene Sloan... One day, you'll believe me. And one day, you'll know I was right all along.

Jonny Gray... Quite possibly the nicest, most genuine guy I have ever met. I'm a better person for knowing you.

Emily Williams... It's my pleasure to call you my friend. I'm so glad we got to know each other.

Karen Sneddon... Being your friend has meant more to me than you'll ever know. You deserve so, so much. I hope you get it.

Helen Fitzgerald... One day, you'll be a millionaire. And you deserve to be! Everyone should read at least one of your books.

Andrew Drennan... Remember me when you collect the Booker. You ARE that good.

Joanne Conachan, Louise Rae, Miss David & Angela Currie... Wonderful, wonderful people, and even nicer for letting me use their names!

Amy Conachan... I'm a far, far better person for knowing you. You really are beautiful in every way.

The guys at Lloyds... Jackie, Julie Anne, Grace, Amanda, Hayley, Theresa, Lynn, Kelly-Anne & Pamela; Caroline,

Martin, Aileen, Colin, Graeme & June; and everyone else I have met on my travels… It's the best job I've ever had, and 99% of that is because of you all. Thank you.

The staff at Costa, Braehead… Thank you for maintaining my caffeine intake during the 7 months it to me to write this thing.

Jenn Cathro and the girls & boys at Costa, Fort Kinnaird… Thank you for being so nice to me when I moved through to Edinburgh.

Andrew Daisley… Two words: Dentist. Genius.

Sarah Lowing, Alfie & Yogi… Thank you for your hospitality and for letting me rent the room! I honestly hope you get what you wish for.

Sarah McKendrick… My knowing you has made me better in almost every way. Whatever you do in life, try not to change. There really is no need.

Louise Lang: Gorgeous, brave and genuinely wonderful in every way. You don't know how much you mean to people, and that just makes you all the more beautiful.

Amanda Brooks… I'm so sorry you hate me. I'm better for knowing you, and I hope we can one day be friends again.

And some special ones now:

Shawn Speakman… You are an inspiration, a fantastic writer, and a great friend. If the world has ANY justice in it, you will be as successful you deserve. Thanks you for everything you have ever done for me.

Ricky Figg… Thank you for allowing me to use "Moon Love" as the cover. You are a truly gifted artist. And everyone should take a look at your work at artgallery.co.uk

Gillian Davidson… Wherever you are. A big, big part of this is yours. I hope you have everything you ever dreamed of, and are beyond happy.

And lastly, Terry & Judine Brooks... My two favourite people in the entire world. I can't imagine life without you, and I owe almost everything to you for making me the person I am today. I'm proud to have you as friends. Thank you.